International bestselling author

Betty Neels

&

Rising star of Harlequin Romance®

Caroline Anderson

bring you...

Two fabulously tender
and deeply emotional stories that will whisk you
into a heartwarming, magical world.

Betty Neels spent her childhood and youth in Devonshire, England, before training as a nurse and midwife. She was an army nursing sister during the war, married a Dutchman and subsequently lived in Holland for fourteen years. She lives with her husband in Dorset, and has a daughter and grandson. Her interests are reading, animals, old buildings and writing. Betty started to write on retirement from nursing, incited by a lady in a library bemoaning the lack of romantic novels. Betty Neels has sold over 35 million copies of her books worldwide.

Look out in November for
ALWAYS AND FOREVER by Betty Neels
Harlequin Romance® #3675

Caroline Anderson has the mind of a butterfly. She's been a nurse, a secretary, a teacher, run her own soft-furnishing business and now she's settled on writing. She says, "I was looking for that elusive something. I finally realized it was variety, and now I have it in abundance. Every book brings new horizons and new friends, and in between books I have learned to be a juggler. My teacher-husband, John, and I have two beautiful daughters, Sarah and Hannah, umpteen pets and several acres of Suffolk, England, that nature tries to reclaim every time we turn our backs!" Caroline also writes for the Medical Romance™ series.

Look out in November for
THE IMPETUOUS BRIDE by Caroline Anderson
Harlequin Romance® #3676

BETTY NEELS
CAROLINE ANDERSON
Marrying a Doctor

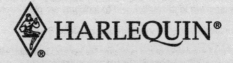

TORONTO • NEW YORK • LONDON
AMSTERDAM • PARIS • SYDNEY • HAMBURG
STOCKHOLM • ATHENS • TOKYO • MILAN • MADRID
PRAGUE • WARSAW • BUDAPEST • AUCKLAND

ISBN 0-373-03674-4

MARRYING A DOCTOR

First North American Publication 2001.

MARRYING A DOCTOR Anthology
Copyright © 2001 by Harlequin Books S.A.

THE DOCTOR'S GIRL
Copyright © 2001 by Betty Neels.

A SPECIAL KIND OF WOMAN
Copyright © 2001 by Caroline Anderson.

Visit us at www.eHarlequin.com

Printed in U.S.A.

CONTENTS

THE DOCTOR'S GIRL   9
Betty Neels

A SPECIAL KIND OF WOMAN   95
Caroline Anderson

For Elizabeth,
my friend and guiding star over the years.

THE DOCTOR'S GIRL
Betty Neels

Dear Reader,

The last time I wrote to you it was Christmastime. Now, when I look out of my study window, our tiny garden is a wealth of green and color with lavender bushes, miniature rose bushes, tobacco plants, poppies and petunias, all growing higgledy-piggledy with buttercups and speedwell sprawling over any space that's left. Untidy, undisciplined, but exactly right for our very small cottage. And indoors it is just as cluttered. Bits and pieces we have brought back when we traveled, presents from friends and family, photos of cats and dogs we have loved, things we cherish for their memories. And that goes for friends, too: times change but some things never will—old friends, old clothes, favorite books...and writing a letter to people you don't know, but who are, all the same, friends. God bless you.

Betty Neels

CHAPTER ONE

MISS MIMI CATTELL gave a low, dramatic moan followed by a few sobbing breaths, but when these had no effect upon the girl standing by the bed she sat up against her pillows, threw one of them at her and screeched, 'Well, don't just stand there, you little fool, phone Dr Gregg this instant. He must come and see me at once. I'm ill; I've hardly slept all night...' She paused to sneeze.

The girl by the bed, a small mousy person, very neat and with a rather plain face enlivened by a pair of vivid green eyes, picked up the pillow.

'Should you first of all try a hot lemon drink and some aspirin?' she suggested in a sensible voice. 'A cold in the head always makes one feel poorly. A day in bed, perhaps?'

The young woman in the bed had flung herself back onto her pillows again. 'Just do as I say for once. I don't pay you to make stupid suggestions. Get out and phone Dr Gregg; he's to come at once.' She moaned again. 'How can I possibly go to the Sinclairs' party this evening...?'

Dr Gregg's receptionist laughed down the phone. 'He's got three more private patients to see and then a clinic at the hospital, and it isn't Dr Gregg—he's gone off for a week's golf—it's his partner. I'll give him the message and you'd better say he'll come as soon as he can. She's not really ill, is she?'

'I don't think so. A nasty head cold...'

The receptionist laughed. 'I don't know why you stay with her.'

9

Loveday put down the phone. She wondered that too, quite often, but it was a case of beggars not being choosers, wasn't it? She had to have a roof over her head, she had to eat and she had to earn money so that she could save for a problematical future. And that meant another year or two working as Mimi Cattell's secretary—a misleading title if ever there was one, for she almost never sent letters, even when Loveday wrote them for her.

That didn't mean that Loveday had nothing to do. Her days were kept nicely busy—the care of Mimi's clothes took up a great deal of time, for what was the point of having a personal maid when Loveday had nothing else to do? Nothing except being at her beck and call each and every day, and if she came home later from a party at night as well.

Loveday, with only an elderly aunt living in a Dartmoor village whom she had never met, made the best of it. She was twenty-four, heartwhole and healthy, and perhaps one day a man would come along and sweep her off her feet. Common sense told her that this was unlikely to be the case, but a girl had to have her dreams...

She went back to the bedroom and found Mimi threshing about in her outsize bed, shouting at the unfortunate housemaid who had brought her breakfast tray.

Loveday prudently took the tray from the girl, who looked as if she was on the point of dropping it, nodded to her to slip away and said bracingly, 'The doctor will come as soon as he can. He has one or two patients to see first.' She made no mention of the clinic. 'If I fetch you a pot of China tea—weak with lemon—it may help you to feel well enough to have a bath and put on a fresh nightie before he comes.'

Mimi brightened. Her life was spent in making herself attractive to men, and perhaps she would feel strong enough to do her face. She said rudely, 'Get the tea, then, and make sure that the lemon's cut wafer-thin...'

Loveday went down to the basement, where Mrs Branch and the housemaid lived their lives. She took the tray with her and, being a practical girl, ate the fingers of toast on it and accepted the mug of tea Mrs Branch offered her. She should have had her breakfast with Mrs Branch and Ellie, but there wasn't much hope of getting it now. Getting Miss Cattell ready for the doctor would take quite a time. She ate the rest of the toast, sliced the lemon and bore a tray, daintily arranged, back upstairs.

Mimi Cattell, a spoilt beauty of society, prepared for the doctor's visit with the same care she took when getting ready for an evening party. 'And you can make the bed while I'm bathing—put some fresh pillowcases on, and don't dawdle...'

It was almost lunchtime by the time she was once more in her bed, carefully made up, wearing a gossamer nightgown, the fairytale effect rather marred by her sniffs. To blow her nose would make it red.

To Loveday's enquiry as to what she would like for lunch she said ill-temperedly that she had no appetite; she would eat something after he had visited her. 'And you'd better wait too; I want you here when he's examining me.'

'I'll fetch a jug of lemonade,' said Loveday, and sped down to the kitchen.

While Ellie obligingly squeezed lemons, she gobbled down soup and a roll; she was going to need all her patience, and the lowering feeling that the doctor might not come for hours was depressing.

She bore the lemonade back upstairs and presently took it down again; it wasn't sweet enough! She was kept occupied after that—opening the heavy curtains a little, then closing them again, longing to open a window and let a little London air into the room when Mimi sprayed herself once more with Chanel No 5. By now Mimi's temper, never long off the boil, was showing signs of erupting. 'He has no right to leave me in such distress,' she fumed. 'I need immediate attention. By the time he gets here I shall have probably got pneumonia. Find my smelling salts and give me the mirror from the dressing table.'

It was getting on for two o'clock when Loveday suggested that a little light lunch might make her employer feel better.

'Rubbish,' snarled Mimi. 'I won't eat a thing until he's examined me. I suppose you want a meal—well, you'll just have to wait.' Her high-pitched voice rose to a screech. 'I don't pay you to sit around and stuff yourself at my expense, you greedy little...'

The door opened by Ellie, and after one look the screech became a soft, patient voice. 'Doctor—at last...'

Mimi put up a hand to rearrange the cunning little curl over one ear to better advantage. 'I don't think we've met,' she purred. To Loveday, she said, 'Pull the curtains and get a chair for the doctor, and then go and stand by the window.' The commands were uttered in a very different voice.

The doctor opened the curtains before Loveday could get to them and pulled up a chair. 'I must introduce myself, Miss Cattell. I am Dr Gregg's partner and for the moment looking after his patients while he is away.'

Mimi said in a wispy voice, 'I thought you would never come. I am rather delicate, you know, and my health often gives cause for concern. My chest...'

She pushed back the bedspread and put a hand on her heart. It was annoying that he had turned away.

'Could we have the window open?' he asked Loveday.

A man after her own heart, thought Loveday, opening

both windows despite Mimi's distressed cry. She would suffer for it later, but now a few lungfuls of London air would be heaven.

From where she stood she had a splendid view of the doctor. He was a tall man, with broad shoulders and fair hair flecked with grey. He was good-looking too, with a rather thin mouth and a splendid nose upon which were perched a pair of spectacles. A pity she couldn't see the colour of his eyes...

Miss Cattell's voice, sharp with impatience, brought her to the bedside. 'Are you deaf?' A remark hastily covered by a fit of sneezing, necessitating the use of a handkerchief and nose-blowing.

The doctor waited patiently until Mimi had resumed her look of patient suffering. He said mildly, 'If you will sit up, I'll listen to your chest.'

He had a deep voice, pleasantly impersonal, and he appeared quite unimpressed by Mimi's charms, ignoring her fluttering breaths and sighs, staring at the wall behind the bed while he used his stethoscope.

'Clear as a bell,' he told her. 'A head cold. I suggest aspirin, hot drinks and some brisk walks in the fresh air—you are quite near Hyde Park, are you not? Eat whatever you fancy and don't drink any alcohol.'

Mimi stared up at him. 'But I'm not well—I'm delicate; I might catch a chill...'

'You have a head cold,' he told her gravely, and Loveday had to admire his bedside manner. 'But you are a healthy woman with a sound pair of lungs. You will be perfectly fit in a couple of days—less, if you do as I suggest.'

Mimi said rudely, 'I'll decide that for myself. When will Dr Gregg be back? I don't know your name...?'

'Andrew Fforde.' He held out a large hand. 'I'm sure you will let me know if you don't make a full recovery.'

Mimi didn't answer. Loveday went to the door with him and said gravely, 'Thank you for coming, Doctor.' She went downstairs with him, along the hall and opened the front door. As he offered a hand and bade her a grave good afternoon she was able to see that his eyes were blue.

A sensible girl, she went first down to the kitchen, where Mrs Branch and Ellie were sitting over a pot of strong tea.

'I've saved you a bite of lunch,' said Mrs Branch, and pushed a mug of tea across the table. 'That weren't Dr Gregg. Ellie says 'e looked a bit of all right?'

'Dr Gregg's partner, and he was nice. Miss Cattell has a head cold.' Mrs Branch handed Loveday a cheese sandwich. 'You'll need that. Well, will she be going out this evening?'

'I should think so,' said Loveday in a cheese-thickened voice.

Miss Cattell was in a splendid rage; the doctor was a fool and she would speak to Dr Gregg about him the moment he was back. 'The man must be struck off,' declared Mimi. 'Does he realise that I am a private patient? And you standing there with the windows wide open, not caring if I live or die.'

Mimi tossed a few pillows around. 'Where have you been? You can get me a gin and tonic…'

'Doctor said no alcohol.'

'You'll do as I say! Make it a large one, and tell Cook to make me an omelette and a salad. I want it now. I shall rest and you can get everything ready for this evening.'

'You are going to the party, Miss Cattell?'

'Of course I am. I don't intend to disappoint my friends. I dare say I'll be home early. I'll ring for you if I am.'

Another half an hour went by while Mimi was rearranged in her bed, offered her omelette and given a second gin and tonic. She finally settled, the windows shut and curtains drawn, for a nap. Loveday, free at last, went to her room on the floor above, kicked off her shoes and got onto the bed. Some days were worse than others...

Miss Cattell was still asleep and snoring when Loveday crept into her room an hour later. In the kitchen once again, for yet another cup of tea, she thankfully accepted Mrs Branch's offer of a casserole kept hot in the oven for her supper. Mimi wouldn't leave the house before half past eight or nine o'clock, and there would be no chance to sit down to her supper before then.

Later, offering more China tea and wafer-thin bread and butter, Loveday was ordered to display a selection of the dresses Miss Cattell intended to wear. She meant to out-shine everyone there and, her cold forgotten, she spent a long time deciding. After the lengthy ritual of bathing, making up her face and doing her hair, and finally being zipped into a flimsy dress which Loveday considered quite indecent, she changed her mind. The flimsy dress was thrown in a heap onto the floor and a striking scarlet outfit was decided upon, which meant that shoes and handbag had to be changed too—and while Loveday was doing that Ellie was ordered to bring another gin and tonic.

Loveday, escorting Mimi to a taxi, had the nasty feeling that the night was going to prove worse than the day had been. She was right; she was wakened at two in the morning by the noisy return of Miss Cattell and several of her friends, who thankfully didn't stay, but that meant she had to go downstairs and help Mimi up to her room.

This was no easy task; Mimi was too drunk to help herself, so that hoisting her upstairs and into her room was a herculean task. Loveday was strong even though she was small, but by the time she had rolled the lady onto her bed she decided that enough was enough. She removed Mimi's shoes, covered her with a light blanket and went back to her own bed.

In a few hours she had to get up again and face Miss Cattell's rage at discovering herself still clad in scarlet crêpe, lying untidily under a blanket. Even worse than that, her dress was torn and stained; Loveday had never heard such language...

When Miss Cattell was once more bathed, her make-up removed, and attired in a satin and lace confection, she declared that she would remain in bed for the rest of the day. 'My cold is still very heavy.' She snorted. 'Cold indeed. That man had no idea of what he was talking about.'

Loveday allowed her thoughts to dwell upon him, and not for the first time. She had liked him. If she were ever ill she would like him to look after her. She frowned. In different surroundings, of course, and in a nightie like Miss Cattell wore. She dismissed the thought as absurd, but as the day wore on it was somehow restful to think about him while Mimi's cross voice went on and on.

On her half-day off, she went to the public library and searched the papers and magazines, looking for jobs. 'Computer skills...knowledge of a foreign language useful...anyone under the age of twenty-five need not apply...kitchen hands willing to work late nights...' A splendid selection, but none of them would do. And they all ended with references required. She didn't think that Miss Cattell would give her a reference, not one which would secure her a job.

As it turned out she was quite right.

It was Mrs Branch who told her that Miss Cattell had quarrelled with the man she had decided she would marry, which was possibly an excuse for her to be even more bad-tempered than usual, and solace herself by filling the house with her friends, going on a shopping spree and staying up until all hours.

It was on the morning after one of Mimi's parties that a bouquet of roses was delivered. They must be arranged at once, she ordered, and there was a particularly lovely vase into which they must go.

Loveday arranged them carefully under her employer's eye and bore them from room to room while Mimi decided where they should go. It was unfortunate that, getting impatient, she turned sharply and knocked the vase and flowers out of Loveday's hands.

'My vase,' she screamed. 'It was worth hundreds of pounds. You careless fool; you'll pay for this...' She gave Loveday a whack over one eye. 'You're fired. Get out now before I send for the police!'

'If anyone sends for the police it will be myself,' said Loveday. 'It was your fault that I dropped the vase and you hit me. I shall leave at once and you can do what you like.' She added, 'I'm very glad to be going.'

Miss Cattell went an ugly red. 'You'll not get a reference from me.'

'I don't expect one. Just a week's wages in lieu of notice.'

Loveday left Mimi standing there and went to her room and packed her few things tidily before going down to the kitchen.

'I'm leaving,' she told Mrs Branch. 'I shall miss you and Ellie; you've both been very kind to me.'

'You're going to have a black eye,' said Mrs Branch. 'Sit down for a second and drink a cup of tea. Where will you go?'

'I don't know...'

'Well, if it's any help, I've a sister who lives near Victoria Park—Spring Blossom Road—she has rooms.

Wait a tick while I write 'er a line. She'll put you up while you sort yerself out.'

Ellie hadn't said a word, but she cut ham sandwiches and wrapped them neatly and gave them to Loveday. It was a kind gesture which almost melted Loveday's icy calm.

She left the house shortly afterwards; she had her week's wages as well as what was owed her in her purse, but she tried not to think of the things Mimi had said to her. It would have been a pleasure to have torn up the money and thrown it at her, but she was going to need every penny of it.

Mrs Branch's sister, Mrs Slade, lived a far cry from Miss Cattell's fashionable house. Loveday, with Mrs Branch's directions written on the back of an envelope, made her way there, lugging her case and shoulder bag. It was a long journey, but there was a lull in the traffic before the lunch hour and the bus queues were short.

Spring Blossom Road couldn't have seen a spring blossom for many years; it was a short, dingy street with small brick houses on either side of it. But it was tolerably quiet and most of the windows had cheerful curtains. It was a relief to find that Mrs Slade had the same kind, cheerful face as her sister. She read Mrs Branch's note and bade Loveday go in.

''Appens I've got the basement vacant,' she told Loveday. 'It's a bit dark, but it's clean.' She smiled suddenly. 'Not what you've been used to, from what I've 'eard. Take it for a week while you find yourself a job. It'll be rent in advance but I'll not overcharge you.'

Then she led the way to the back of the house, told Loveday to sit down at the kitchen table and offered tea.

'That's a nasty eye you've got there—Miss Cattell had one of her tantrums? My sister only stays until Ellie gets married. I don't 'old with these idle folk with nothing better to do than get nasty.'

The tea was hot and strong and sweet and Loveday felt better. This was something which had been bound to happen sooner or later; she should count herself lucky that Mrs Branch had been so kind and helpful and that she had two weeks' wages in her bag.

She went with Mrs Slade to inspect the basement presently. It was a small room below street level, so that the only view was of feet passing the window. But there was a divan bed, a table, two chairs and a shabby armchair by a small electric fire. There was a sink in one corner, and a small door which led to the neglected strip of back garden. 'Outside lav. Nice and handy for you,' explained Mrs Slade. ''Ere's a key, and you'd better pop down to the corner and get yourself some food. There is a gas ring by the sink so you can cook if you want to.'

So Loveday went to the small shops at the end of the road and bought eggs, butter, tea and a bottle of milk. She still had the ham sandwiches, which would do very nicely for her supper...

She was a sensible girl, and now that her boats were burnt behind her she was cheerfully optimistic. Loveday ate her sandwiches, drank more tea and contrived to wash at the sink before venturing cautiously into the back garden to find the loo. And then, tired by such an eventful day, she got onto the divan and went to sleep. Her eye was painful but there was no mirror for her to inspect it, only her tiny powder compact which was quite inadequate.

It was raining in the morning and there was the first chill of autumn in the air. Loveday boiled an egg, counted her money and sat down to plan her day. She couldn't remember her mother and father, who had both died in a rail crash while she was still a toddler, but the stern aunt who had brought her up had instilled in her a number of useful adages. 'Strike while the iron is hot' was one of them, and Loveday intended to do just that.

She would visit the nearest job centre, the public library, and make a round of the adverts in the small shop windows. That would be a start. But before she did, she allowed her thoughts to wander a little. Miss Cattell would certainly insist on Dr Gregg visiting her, and if she did that she would be able to complain about Dr Ffelde. She hoped she would not; they hadn't exchanged two words and yet she had the firm feeling that she knew him well.

Her eye was painful and almost closed, and, had she but known it, was the reason why the job centre lady wasn't very helpful. She had to admit that it looked rather awful when she caught sight of it in a passing shop window. Tomorrow, if it wasn't better, she would go to the nearest hospital and get something for it. Next she applied for a job as a waitress in a large, noisy café and was told to stop wasting time by the proprietor.

'Oo's going to order from a girl with an eye like that? Been in a fight, 'ave yer?'

The next morning she caught a bus to the hospital, a mile away. It was a vast Victorian building, its Casualty already overflowing. Since Loveday's eye wasn't an urgent case, she was told to sit on one of the crowded benches and wait.

The benches didn't seem any less crowded; rather the opposite. At midday she got a cup of coffee and a roll from the canteen and then settled down to wait again. She was still waiting when Ffelde, on his way to take a clinic in outpatients, took a short cut there through Casualty. He was late and he hardly noticed the sea of faces looking hopefully at him. He was almost by the end doors when he caught sight of Loveday, or rather he caught sight of the black eye, now a rainbow of colours and swollen shut.

It was the mouse-like girl who had been with that abominable Miss Cattell. Why was she here in the East end of London with an eye like that? He had felt an instant and quite unexpected liking for her when he had seen her, and now he realised that he was glad to have found her again, even if the circumstances were peculiar. He must find out about her... He was through the doors by now and encircled by his clerk, his houseman and Sister, already touchy because he was late.

Of course by the time he had finished his clinic the Casualty benches were almost empty and there was no sign of her. Impelled by some feeling he didn't examine, he went to Casualty and asked to see the cases for the day. 'A young lady with a black eye,' he told the receptionist. 'Have you her address? She is concerned with one of my patients.'

The receptionist was helpful; she liked him, for he was polite and friendly and good-looking. 'Miss Loveday West, unemployed, gave an address in Spring Blossom Road. That's turn left from here and half a mile down the road. Had her eye treated; no need to return.'

He thanked her nicely, then got into his car and drove back to his consulting room. He had two patients to see and he was already late...

There was no reason why he should feel this urge to see her again; he had smiled briefly, they had exchanged goodbyes on the doorstep and that was all. But if the opportunity should occur...

Which it did, and far more rapidly than he anticipated.

Waiting for him when he reached his rooms on the following morning was Miss Priss, his receptionist-secretary. She was a thin lady of middle years, with a wispy voice and a tendency to crack her knuckles when agitated, but nevertheless she was his mainstay and prop. Even in her agitation she remembered to wish him a good morning before explaining that she had had bad news; she needed to go home at once—her mother had been taken ill and there was no one else...

Dr Fforde waited until she had drawn breath. 'Of course you must go at once. Take a taxi and stay as long as you wish to. Dr Gregg will be back today, and I'm not busy. We shall manage very well. Have you sufficient money? Is there anyone you wish to telephone?'

'Yes, thank you, and there is nobody to phone.'

'Then get a taxi and I'll ask Mrs Betts to bring you a cup of tea.'

Mrs Betts, who kept the various consulting rooms clean, was like a sparrow, small and perky and pleased to take a small part in any dramatic event.

Miss Priss, fortified by what Mrs Betts called her 'special brew', was seen on her way, and then Dr Fforde sat down at his desk and phoned the first agency in the phone book. Someone would come, but not until the afternoon. It was fortunate that Mr Jackson, in the rooms above him, was away for the day and his secretary agreed to take Miss Priss's place for the morning...

The girl from the agency was young, pretty and inefficient. By the end of the next day Dr Fforde, a man with a well-controlled temper, was having difficulty in holding it in check. He let himself into his small mews house, tucked away behind a terrace of grand Georgian mansions, and went from the narrow hall into the kitchen, where his housekeeper, Mrs Duckett, was standing at the table making pastry.

She took a look at his tired face. 'A nice cuppa is what you're needing, sir. Just you go along to your study and

I'll bring it in two shakes of a lamb's tail. Have you had a busy day?'

He told her about Miss Priss. 'Then you'll have to find someone as good as her to take her pace,' said Mrs Duckett.

He went to his study, lifted Mrs Duckett's elderly cat off his chair and sat down with her on his knee. He had letters to write, a mass of paperwork, patients' notes to read, and the outline of a lecture he was to give during the following week to prepare. He loved his work, and with Miss Priss to see to his consulting room and remind him of his daily appointments he enjoyed it. But not, he thought savagely, if he had to endure her replacement—the thought of another day of her silly giggle and lack of common sense wouldn't bear contemplating.

Something had to be done, and even while he thought that he knew the answer.

Loveday had gone back from the hospital knowing that it wasn't much use looking for work until her eye looked more normal. It would take a few days, the casualty officer had told her, but her eye hadn't been damaged. She should bathe it frequently and come back if it didn't improve within a day or so.

So she had gone back to the basement room with a tin of beans for lunch and the local paper someone had left on the bench beside her. It was a bit late for lunch, so she'd had an early tea with the beans and gone to bed.

A persistent faint mewing had woken her during the small hours, and when she'd opened the door into the garden a very small, thin cat had slunk in, to crouch in a corner. Loveday had shut the door, offered milk, and watched the small creature gulp it down, so she'd crumbled bread into more milk and watched that disappear too.

It was a miserable specimen of a cat, with bedraggled fur and bones and it had been terrified. She'd got back into bed, and presently the little beast had crept onto the old quilt and gone to sleep.

'So now I've got a cat,' Loveday had said, and went off to sleep too.

This morning her eye was better. It was still hideously discoloured but at least she could open it a little. She dressed while she talked soothingly to the cat and presently, leaving it once more crouching there in the corner, she went to ask Mrs Slade if she knew if it belonged to anybody.

'Bless you, no, my dear. People who had it went away and left it behind.'

'Then would you mind very much if I had it? When I find work and perhaps have to leave here, I could take it with me.'

'And why not? No one else will be bothered with the little creature. Yer eye is better.'

'I went to the hospital. They said it would be fine in another day or two.'

Mrs Slade looked her up and down. 'Got enough to eat?'

'Oh, yes,' said Loveday. 'I'm just going to the shops now.'

She bought milk and bread and more beans, and a tin of rice pudding because the cat so obviously needed nourishing, plus cat food and a bag of apples going cheap. Several people stopped to say what a nasty eye she had.

She and the cat had bread and butter and milk pudding for lunch, and the cat perked up enough to make feeble attempts to wash while Loveday counted her money and did sums. The pair of them got into the chair presently and dozed until it was time to boil the kettle and make tea while the cat had the last of the rice pudding.

It was bordering on twilight when there was a thump on the door. The cat got under the divan and after a moment there was another urgent thump on the door. Loveday went to open it.

'Hello,' said Dr Fforde. 'May I come in?'

He didn't wait for her to close her astonished mouth but came in and shut the door. He said pleasantly, 'That's a nasty eye.'

There was no point in pretending she didn't know who he was. Full of pleasure at the sight of him, and imbued with the feeling that it was perfectly natural for him to come and see her, she smiled widely.

'How did you know where I was?'

'I saw you at the hospital. I've come to ask a favour of you.'

'Me? A favour?' She glanced round her. 'But I'm hardly in a position to grant a favour.'

'May we sit down?' And when she was in the armchair he sat carefully on the old kitchen chair opposite. 'But first, may I ask why you are here? You were with Miss Cattell, were you not?'

'Well, yes, but I dropped a vase, a very expensive one...'

'So she slapped you and sent you packing?'

'Yes.'

'So why are you here?'

'Mrs Branch, she is Miss Cattell's cook, sent me here because Mrs Slade who owns it is her sister and I had nowhere to go.'

The doctor took off his specs, polished them, and put them back on. He observed pleasantly, 'There's a cat under the bed.'

'Yes, I know. He's starving. I'm going to look after him.'

The doctor sighed silently. Not only was he about to

take on a mousy girl with a black eye but a stray cat too. He must be mad!

'The favour I wish to ask of you: my receptionist at my consulting rooms has had to return home at a moment's notice; would you consider taking her place until she returns? It isn't a difficult job—opening the post, answering the phone, dealing with patients. The hours are sometimes odd, but it is largely a matter of common sense.'

Loveday sat and looked at him. Finally, since he was sitting there calmly waiting for her to speak, she said, 'I can type and do shorthand, but I don't understand computers. I don't think it would do because of my eye—and I can't leave the cat.'

'I don't want you to bother with computers, but typing would be a bonus, and you have a nice quiet voice and an unobtrusive manner—both things which patients expect and do appreciate. As for the cat, I see no reason why you shouldn't keep it.'

'Isn't it a long way from here to where you work? I do wonder why you have come here. I mean, there must be any number of suitable receptionists from all those agencies.'

'Since Miss Priss went two days ago I have endured the services of a charming young lady who calls my patients "dear" and burst into tears because she broke her nail on the typewriter. She is also distractingly pretty, which is hardly an asset for a job such as I'm offering you. I do not wish to be distracted, and my patients have other things on their minds besides pretty faces.'

Which meant, when all was said and done, that Loveday had the kind of face no one would look at twice. Background material, that's me, thought Loveday.

'And where will I live?'

'There is a very small flat on the top floor of the house

where I have my rooms. There are two other medical men there, and of course the place is empty at night. You could live there—and the cat, if you wish.'

'You really mean that?'

All at once he looked forbidding. 'I endeavour to say what I mean, Miss West.'

She made haste to apologise. 'What I really mean is that you don't know anything about me and I don't know anything about you. We're strangers, aren't we? And yet here you are, offering me a job,' she added hastily, in case he had second thoughts. 'It sounds too good to be true.'

'Nevertheless, it is a genuine offer of work—and do not forget that only the urgency of my need for adequate help has prompted me to offer you the job. You are at liberty to leave if you should wish to do so, providing you give me adequate time to find a replacement. If Miss Priss should return she would, of course, resume her work; that is a risk for you.' He smiled suddenly. 'We are both taking a risk, but it is to our advantage that we should help each other.'

Such terms of practicability and common sense made the vague doubts at the back of Loveday's head melt away. She had had no future, and now all at once security—even if temporary—was being handed her on a plate.

'All right,' said Loveday. 'I'll come.'

'Thank you. Could you be ready if I fetch you at half past eight tomorrow morning? My first patient is at eleven-thirty, which will give you time to find your way around.'

He stood up and held out a hand. 'I think we shall deal well with each other, Miss West.'

She put her hand in his and felt the reassuring firmness of it.

'I'll be ready—and the cat. You haven't forgotten the cat?''

'No, I haven't forgotten.'

CHAPTER TWO

LOVEDAY went to see Mrs Slade then, and in answer to that lady's doubtful reception of her news assured her that Dr Fforde was no stranger.

'Well, yer a sensible girl, but if you need an 'elping 'and yer know where to come.'

Loveday thanked her. 'I'll write to you,' she said, 'and I'll write to Mrs Branch too. I think it's a job I can manage, and it will be nice to have somewhere to live where I can have the cat.'

She said goodbye and went back to the basement, and, since a celebration was called for, she gave the cat half the cat meat and boiled two eggs.

In the morning she was a bit worried that the cat might try and escape, but the little beast was still too weak and weary to do more than cling to her when the doctor arrived. His good morning was businesslike as he popped her into the car, put her case into the boot and got in and drove away.

He was still glad to see her, but he had a busy day ahead of him and a day was only so long...

Loveday, sensing that, made no effort to talk, but sat clutching the cat, savouring the delight of being driven in a Bentley motor car.

His rooms were in a house in a quiet street, one in a terrace of similar houses. He ushered her into the narrow hall with its lofty ceiling and up the handsome staircase at its end. There were several doors on the landing, and as they started up the next flight he nodded to the end one.

'I'm in the end room. We'll go to your place first.'

They went up another flight of stairs past more doors and finally up a small staircase with a door at the top.

The doctor took a key from a pocket and opened it. It gave directly into a small room, its window opening onto the flat roof of the room below. There were two doors but he didn't open them.

'The porter will bring up your case. And I asked him to stock up your cupboard. I suggest you feed the cat and leave the window shut and then come down to my room. Ten minutes?'

He had gone, leaving her to revolve slowly, trying to take it all in. But not for long. Ten minutes didn't give her much time. She opened one of the doors and found a small room with just space for a narrow bed, a table, a mirror and a chair. It had a small window and the curtains were pretty. Still with the cat tucked under her arm, she opened the other door. It was a minute kitchen, and between it and the bedroom was an even smaller shower room.

Loveday sucked in her breath like a happy child and went to the door to see who was there. It was the porter with her case.

'Todd's the name, miss. I'm here all day until seven o'clock, so do ask if you need anything. Dr Fforde said you've got a cat. I'll bring up a tray and suchlike before I go. There's enough in the cupboard to keep you going for a bit.'

She thanked him, settled the cat on the bed and offered it food, then tidied her hair, powdered her nose and went down to the first floor, the door key in her pocket. She should have been feeling nervous, but there hadn't been time.

She knocked and walked in. This was the waiting room, she supposed, all restful greys and blues, and with one or two charming flower paintings on the walls. There was a desk in one corner with a filing cabinet beside it.

'In here,' said Dr Fforde, and she went through a half-open door to the room beyond where he sat at his desk. He got up as she went in.

He noticed with satisfaction that she looked very composed, as neat as a new pin, and the black eye was better, allowing for a glint of vivid green under the lid.

'I'll take you round and show you where everything is, and we will have coffee while I explain your work. There should be time after that for you to go around on your own, just to check things. As I told you, there are few skills required—only a smiling face for all the patients and the ability to cope with simple routine.'

He showed her the treatment room leading from his consulting room. 'Nurse Paget comes about ten o'clock, unless I've a patient before then. She isn't here every day, so she will explain her hours to you when you meet her. Now, this is the waiting room, which is our domain.'

Her duties were simple. Even at such short notice she thought that she would manage well enough, and there would be no one there in the afternoon so she would have time to go over her duties again. There would be three patients after five o'clock, he told her.

'Now, your hours of work. You have an early-morning start—eight o'clock—an hour for lunch, between twelve and one, and tea when you have half an hour to spare during the afternoon. You'll be free to leave at five o'clock, but I must warn you that frequently I have an evening patient and you would need to be here. You have half-day on Saturday and all Sunday free, but Miss Priss came in on Saturday mornings to get everything ready for Monday. Can you cope with that?'

'Yes,' said Loveday. 'You will tell me if I don't do everything as you like it?'

'Yes. Now, salary...' He mentioned a sum which made her blink the good eye.

'Too much,' said Loveday roundly. 'I'm living rent-free, remember.'

She encountered an icy blue stare. 'Allow me to make my own decisions, Miss West.'

She nodded meekly and said, 'Yes, Doctor,' but there was nothing meek about the sparkle in her eye. She would have liked to ask him to stop calling her Miss West with every breath, but since she was in his employ she supposed that she would have to answer to anything she felt he wished to call her.

That night, lying in her bed with the cat wrapped in one of her woolies curled up at her feet, Loveday, half asleep, went over the day. The two morning patients had been no problem; she had greeted them by name and ushered them in and out again, dealt with their appointments and filed away their notes and when the doctor, with a brief nod, had gone away, she had locked the door and come upstairs to her new home.

Todd had left everything necessary for the cat's comfort outside the door. She had opened the window onto the flat roof, arranged everything to her satisfaction and watched the cat creep cautiously through the half-open window and then back again. She'd fed him then, and made herself a cheese sandwich and a cup of coffee from the stock of food neatly stacked away in the kitchen.

The afternoon she had spent prowling round the consulting rooms, checking and re-checking; for such a magnificent wage she intended to be perfect...

The doctor had returned shortly before the first of his late patients, refused the tea she had offered to make him, and when the last one had gone he'd gone too, observing quietly that she appeared to have settled in nicely and bidding her goodnight. She had felt hurt that he hadn't said more than that, but had consoled herself with the thought that he led a busy life and although he had given her a job and a roof over her head that was no reason why he should concern himself further.

She had spent a blissful evening doing sums and making a list of all the things she would like to buy. It was a lengthy list...

Dr Fforde had taken himself off home. There was no doubt about it, Loveday had taken to her new job like a duck to water. His patients, accustomed to Miss Priss's austere politeness, had been made aware of the reason for her absence, and had expressed polite concern and commented on the suitability of her substitute. She might not have Miss Priss's presence but she had a pleasant manner and a quiet voice which didn't encroach...

He'd had an urgent call from the hospital within ten minutes of his return to his home. His work had taken over then, and for the time being, at least, he had forgotten her.

Loveday slept soundly with the cat curled up on her feet, and woke with the pleasant feeling that she was going to enjoy her day. She left the cat to potter onto the roof, which it did, while she showered and dressed and got breakfast. She wondered who had had the thoughtfulness to get several tins of cat food as she watched the little beast scoff its meal.

'You're beginning to look like a cat,' she told him, 'and worthy of a name.' When he paused to look at her, she added, 'I shall call you Sam, and I must say that it is nice to have someone to talk to.'

She made him comfortable on the woolly, left the window open and went down to the consulting room.

It was still early, and there was no one about except the porter, who wished her a cheerful good morning. 'Put your rubbish out on a Friday,' he warned her. 'And will you be wanting milk?'

'Yes, please. Does the milkman call?'

'He does. I'll get him to leave an extra pint and I'll put it outside your door.'

She thanked him and unlocked the waiting room door. For such a magnificent sum the doctor deserved the very best attention; she dusted and polished, saw to the flowers in their vases, arranged the post just so on his desk, got out the patients' notes for the day and put everything ready to make coffee. That done, she went and sat by the open window and watched the quiet street below. When the Bentley whispered to a halt below she went and sat down behind her desk in the corner of the room.

The doctor, coming in presently, glanced at her as he wished her a brisk good morning and sighed with silent relief. She hadn't been putting on a show yesterday; she really was composed and capable, sitting there sedately, ready to melt into the background until she was wanted.

He paused at his door. 'Any problems? You are quite comfortable upstairs?'

'Yes, thank you, and there are no problems. Would you like coffee? It'll only take a minute.'

'Please. Would you bring it in?'

Since she made no effort to attract attention to herself he forgot her, absorbed in his patients, but remembered as he left to visit those who were housebound or too ill to come and see him, to wish her good morning and advise her that he would be back during the afternoon.

Loveday, eating her lunchtime sandwich, leaning out of

the window watching Sam stretched out in the autumn sunshine, told the cat about the morning's work, the patients who had come, and the few bad moments she had had when she had mislaid some notes.

'I found them, luckily,' she explained to him. 'I can't afford to slip up, can I, Sam? I don't wish Miss Priss to be too worried about her mother, but I do hope she won't come back until I've saved some money and found a job where you'll be welcome.'

Sam paused in his wash and brush-up and gave her a look. He was going to be a handsome cat, but he wasn't young any more, so a settled life would suit him down to the ground. He conveyed his feelings with a look, and Loveday said, 'Yes, I know, Sam. But I'll not part with you, I promise.'

At the end of the week she found an envelope with her wages on her desk, and when she thanked the doctor he said, 'I'll be away for the weekend. You'll be here in the morning? Take any phone calls, and for anything urgent you can reach me at the number on my desk. Set the answering-machine when you leave. I have a patient at half past nine on Monday morning.' At the door he paused. 'I hope you have a pleasant weekend.'

At noon on Saturday she locked the consulting rooms and went to her little flat. With Sam on her lap she made a shopping list, ate her lunch and, bidding him to be a good boy, set off to the nearest shops. The porter had told her that five minutes' walk away there were shops which should supply her needs. 'Nothing posh,' he said. 'Been there for years, they have, very handy, too.'

She soon found them, tucked away behind the rather grand houses: the butcher, the baker, the greengrocer, all inhabiting small and rather shabby shops, but selling everything she had on her list. There was a newsagent too,

selling soft drinks, chocolates and sweets, and with a shelf
of second-hand books going cheap.

Loveday went back to her flat and unpacked her carrier
bags. She still wasn't sure when she could get out during
the day, and had prudently stocked up with enough food
to last for several days. That done, she sat down to her tea
and made another list—clothes, this time. They were a pipe
dream at the moment, but there was no harm in considering
what she would buy once she had saved up enough money
to spend some of it.

It was very quiet in the house. Todd had locked up and
gone home, and the place would be empty now until he
came again around six o'clock on Monday morning. Loveday wasn't nervous; indeed she welcomed the silence after
Miss Cattell's voice raised unendingly in demands and
complaints. She washed her hair and went to bed early,
with Sam for company.

She went walking on Sunday, to St James's Park and
then Hyde Park, stopping for coffee on the way. It was a
chilly day but she was happy. To be free, with money in
her purse and a home to go back to—what more could she
ask of life? she reflected. Well, quite a bit, she conceded—
a husband, children and a home…and to be loved.

'A waste of time,' said Loveday, with no one to hear
her. 'Who would want to marry me in the first place and
how would I ever meet him?'

She walked on briskly. He would have to love her even
though she wasn't pretty, and preferably have enough
money to have a nice home and like children. Never mind
what he looked like… She paused. Yes, she did mind—he
would need to be tall and reassuringly large, and she
wouldn't object to him wearing specs on his handsome
nose…

'You're being ridiculous,' said Loveday. 'Just because he's the only man who has spoken to you for years.'

She took herself off back home and had a leisurely lunch—a lamb chop, sprouts and a jacket potato, with a tub of yoghurt for pudding—and then sat in the little armchair with Sam on her lap and read the Sunday paper from front to back. And then tea, and later supper and bed.

'Some would call it a dull day, but we've enjoyed every minute of it,' she told Sam.

The week began well. The nurse, whom she seldom saw, had treated her with coolness at first, and then, realising that Loveday presented no risk to her status, became casually friendly. As for Dr Fforde, he treated her with the brisk, friendly manner which she found daunting. But such treatment was only to be expected....

It was almost the end of the week when he came earlier than usual to the consulting rooms. She gave him coffee and, since she was for the moment idle, paused to tell him that Sam had turned into a handsome cat. 'And he's very intelligent,' she added chattily. 'You really should come up and see him some time...'

The moment she had uttered them she wished the words unsaid. The doctor's cool, 'I'm glad to hear that he has made such a good recovery,' uttered in a dismissive voice sent the colour into her cheeks. Of course the very idea of his climbing the stairs to her little flat to look at the cat was ridiculous. As though he had the slightest interest...

She buried her hot face in the filing cabinet. Never, *never*, she vowed, would she make that mistake again.

Dr Fforde, watching her, wondered how best to explain to her that visiting her at the flat would cause gossip—friendly, no doubt, but to be avoided. He decided to say nothing, but asked her in his usual grave way to telephone the hospital and say that he might be half an hour late.

'Mrs Seward has an appointment after the last patient. She is not a patient, so please show her in at once.'

The last patient had barely been shown out when Mrs Seward arrived. She was tall, slender, with a lovely face, skilfully made up, and wearing the kind of clothes Loveday dreamed of. She had a lovely smile, too.

'Hello—you're new, aren't you? What's happened to Miss Priss? Has Andrew finished? I'm a bit early.'

'Mrs Seward? Dr Fforde's expecting you.'

Loveday opened his door and stood aside for Mrs Seward to go in. Before she closed it she heard him say, 'Margaret—this is delightful.'

'Andrew, it's been so long...' was Mrs Seward's happy reply.

Loveday went back to her desk and got out the afternoon patients' notes. That done, she entered their names and phone numbers into the daily diary. It was time for her to go to her lunch, but she supposed that she should stay; they would go presently and she could lock up. He would be at the hospital during the afternoon, and there were no more patients until almost four o'clock.

She didn't have long to wait. They came out together presently, and the doctor stopped at the desk and asked her to lock up. 'And since the first patient is at four o'clock there's no need for you to come back until three.'

His voice was as kind as his smile. Mrs Seward smiled too. On their way down to the car she said, 'I like your receptionist. A mouse with green eyes.'

The extra hour or so for lunch wasn't to be ignored. Loveday gobbled a sandwich, fed Sam, and went shopping, returning with her own simple needs and weighed down by tins of cat food and more books. She had seen that the funny little shop squeezed in between the grocer and the butcher sold just about everything and had noticed some small, cheap radios. On pay day, she promised herself, she would buy one. And the greengrocer had had a bucketful of chrysanthemums outside his shop; they perhaps weren't quite as fresh as they might have been, but they would add a cheerful splash of colour in the flat.

The doctor arrived back five minutes before his patient, accepted the cup of tea she offered him and, when the last patient of the afternoon had gone, bade her goodnight without loss of time.

'They'll go out this evening,' said Loveday aloud. 'To one of those restaurants with little lamps on the tables. And then they'll go dancing. She's quite beautiful. They make a handsome pair.'

She locked up with her usual care and went upstairs to give Sam his supper and herself a pot of tea. She would have a pleasant evening, she told herself: an omelette for her supper and then a peaceful hour with one of the second-hand books.

'I'm becoming an old maid,' said Loveday.

There was news of Miss Priss in the morning; her mother was recovering from her stroke but must stay in hospital for another ten days. After that she would return home and be nursed by Miss Priss and a helper. There was every chance that she would recover, and then Miss Priss would be able to return to work once arrangements for her mother's comfort could be made.

The doctor told Loveday this without going into details, and although she was sorry for Miss Priss and her mother, she couldn't help feeling relief. She had known that sooner or later Miss Priss would be back, but the longer she could stay the more money she could save, and with some experience and a reference from the doctor she would have a better chance of finding work. She must remember, she told herself, to curb her tongue and not talk about herself or Sam.

As a result of this resolution the doctor was at first faintly amused and then puzzled at her wooden politeness towards him. She had become in the short time she had been working for him almost as efficient as Miss Priss; she was discreet, pleasantly attentive to his patients, willing to come early and work late if need be, and disappeared to her little flat so quietly that he barely noticed her going. And always there when he arrived in the mornings. It was what he expected and what he paid her for, but all the same he now had a vague sense of disquiet, so that he found himself thinking about her very frequently.

A few days later she went down rather earlier; there were more patients than usual today. The doctor would expect everything to be ready for them.

There was a man on the landing outside the consulting rooms, standing easily, hands in pockets, looking out of the landing window. He turned round to look at her as she reached the door.

He smiled at her and said good morning. 'I hoped someone would come soon. I'd love a cup of coffee.' At her surprised look, he added, 'Oh, it's quite all right, Andrew won't mind.'

When she still stood there, looking at him, he added impatiently, 'Open up, dear girl.'

'Certainly not,' said Loveday. 'I don't know who you are, and even if you told me I'm not to know whether it's the truth. I'm so sorry, but if you want to see the doctor then you should come back at nine o'clock.'

She put the key in the lock. 'I have no intention of letting you in.'

She whisked herself inside, locked the door again and

left him there. He had been sure of himself, demanding coffee, behaving as if he knew the doctor, but he could so easily be intent on skulduggery...

She set about her morning chores and had everything just as the doctor liked and the coffee ready when he came in.

The young man was with him and they were both laughing.

The doctor's good morning was said in his usual quiet manner, but his companion told Loveday, 'You see, I am a bona fide caller. Are you not remorseful at your treatment of me? And I only asked to be let in and given coffee.'

'You could have been a thief,' said Loveday.

'Quite right, Loveday,' interposed the doctor. 'You did the right thing and, since my cousin hasn't the good grace to introduce himself, I must do it for him. Charles Fforde, this is Miss Loveday West, who is my most efficient receptionist.'

Charles offered a hand, and after a tiny pause she shook it.

'What happened to Miss Prissy?'

'I'll tell you about her. Come into my room. There is time for coffee, but you must go away before my patients arrive.' The doctor opened his door. 'I should be free about one o'clock; we'll have lunch together.'

Loveday fetched the coffee. Charles was much younger than the doctor—more her own age, she supposed. He was good-looking too, and well dressed. She thought uneasily that he was very like Miss Cattell's men-friends, only younger. On the other hand he was the doctor's cousin, and he, in her view, was beyond reproach.

Charles didn't stay long, and on his way out he paused by her desk.

'Did anyone ever tell you that you have very beautiful

eyes? The rest of you is probably charming, though hardly breathtaking, but the eyes…!'

He bent down and kissed the end of her nose.

'Till we meet again,' he told her, and reached the door in time to hold it open for the first patient.

No one had ever told Loveday that her eyes were beautiful. She savoured that for the rest of the day and tried to forget his remark about not being breathtaking. It had been so long since anyone had passed a remark about her appearance that she found it hard to ignore.

That evening, getting ready for bed, she examined her face carefully. 'Hardly breathtaking' was a kind way of saying plain…

All the same she took extra pains with her face and hair in the morning, and made plans to buy a new dress on Saturday afternoon.

If she had hoped to see Charles the next day she was disappointed. There was no sign of him, and Dr Fforde, beyond his usual pleasant greeting, had nothing to say. All the same, she spent Saturday afternoon searching for a dress. It had to be something that would last. She found it after much searching: a navy blue wool crêpe, well cut and elegant, with the kind of neckline which could be dressed up by a pretty scarf. She bore it back and tried it on with Sam for a rather bored audience.

And on Monday morning she wore it to work.

Dr Fforde, wishing her his usual pleasant good morning noticed it immediately. It was undoubtedly suitable for her job, but it hardly enhanced her appearance. Her pretty mousy hair and those green eyes should be complemented by rich greens and russet, not buried in navy blue. He thought it unlikely that she had many friends, and perhaps none close enough to point this out to her. A pity. He sat down at his desk and started to go through his post.

It was Charles who voiced this same opinion when he came again during the week. He sauntered in after the last of the morning patients had gone and stopped at her desk.

'A new dress', he said as he eyed her up and down in a friendly fashion. 'In excellent taste too, dear girl, but why hide your charms behind such a middle-aged colour? You should be wearing pink and blue and emerald-green, and all the colours of the rainbow…'

'Not if she is to remain my receptionist,' said the doctor from his door, so that Loveday's wide smile at the sight of Charles was quenched. She contrived to look faintly amused, although her eyes sparkled green fire. The phone rang then and she turned to answer it, and the two men went into the consulting room together.

She had been delighted to see Charles, and although he didn't like the new dress he had said it was hiding her charms—which sounded old-fashioned but pleasant. And then Dr Fforde had to spoil it all. Who knew what Charles would have said if they had been left alone?

Loveday, a level-headed girl, realised that she was behaving in a way quite unlike her usual self-contained self. 'Which won't do,' she muttered as the phone rang again. And no one could have looked more efficient and at the same time inconspicuous than she did as Dr Fforde and Charles came into the room again.

'I shall be at the hospital until five o'clock,' the doctor told her. 'Have the afternoon off, but please be here by half past four.'

So Loveday had a leisurely lunch and decided to do some more shopping. She didn't need much, but she seldom had the chance to go out during the day and it was a bright day even if chilly. She got into her jacket—navy blue again, and bought to last—and with her shopping basket over one arm went out.

She had only gone a few yards down the street when she met Charles.

He took her arm. 'How about a walk in the park and tea? It's a splendid afternoon for exercise.'

She didn't try to conceal her pleasure at seeing him again. 'It sounds lovely, but I'm going shopping.'

'You can shop any day of the week.' He had tucked one arm into hers. 'Half an hour's brisk walk, then tea, and then if you must shop...'

'I have to be back by half past four.'

'Yes, yes. That's almost three hours away.'

He was laughing at her and, despite her good resolutions, she smiled back. 'A walk would be nice...'

He was an amusing companion and, bored with having nothing much to do for the moment, he found it intriguing to attract this rather sedate girl who had no idea how to make the most of herself. He had charm and a light-hearted way of talking, uncaring that he rarely meant a word of what he uttered. Those who knew him well joined in his cheerful banter and didn't take it seriously, but Loveday wasn't to know that...

He took her to a small café near the park, plied her with cream cakes and called her dear girl, and when they parted outside the consulting rooms he begged her to see him again. He touched the tip of her nose very gently as he spoke and his smile was such that she agreed at once.

'But I'm only free on Saturday afternoons and Sundays.'

'Sunday it shall be. We will drive into the country and walk and talk and eat at some village pub.' He turned away. 'Ten o'clock?'

'He didn't wait for her reply, which just for a moment

she found disturbing, but she brushed that aside. A day out in his company would be lovely.

Dr Fforde, coming back just before five o'clock, wondered what had given Loveday a kind of inner glow; she was no longer insignificant, and her ordinary face was alight with happiness.

He asked, 'You enjoyed your afternoon?'

'Yes, thank you, Doctor.' Her beaming smile included him in her happiness, and for some reason that made him uneasy.

At breakfast on Sunday morning, Loveday explained to Sam that she would be away for the day. 'Well, most of it, I hope.' She added, 'But I won't be late home.' She kissed his elderly head. 'Be a good boy.'

Charles had said a drive into the country and a village pub. Her jacket and a skirt would be quite suitable; she would wear her good shoes and the pale blue sweater...

She was ready and waiting when she heard the silence of the quiet street disturbed by the prolonged blowing of his car's horn. She reached his car just as he was about to blow it again. 'Oh, hush,' she begged him. 'It's Sunday morning.'

He had looked faintly impatient, but now he laughed. 'So it is and we have the whole day before us.' He leaned across and opened the car door. 'Jump in.'

His car was a sports model, scarlet and flashy. She suppressed the instant thought that Dr Fforde's car was more to her liking and settled down beside Charles.

'It's a lovely morning,' she began.

'Marvellous, darling, but don't chatter until we are out of London.'

So she sat quietly, happy just to be there, sitting beside

him, leaving the streets and rows of houses behind for a few hours.

He drove south, through Sevenoaks, and she wondered where they were going. They were well clear of London by now, but he had nothing much to say until he asked suddenly, 'Have you any idea where we're going?'

'No, except that it's south—towards the coast.'

'Brighton, darling. Plenty to do and see there.'

She had expected a day in the country—he had mentioned a country pub. Surely Brighton wasn't much different from London? But what did it matter where they went? She was happy in his company and he made her laugh...

He parked at the seafront and they had coffee and then walked, first by the sea and then through the town, stopping to look at the shop windows in the Lanes. Charles promised her that the next time they came he would take her to the Pavilion. They had lunch in a fashionable pub and then walked again, and if it wasn't quite what she had expected it didn't really matter. She was having a lovely day out and Charles was a delightful companion, teasing her a little, letting her see that he liked her, and telling her that he had never met a girl quite like her before. Loveday, hopelessly ignorant of the fashionable world, believed every word of it.

They drove back to London after a splendid tea in one of the seafront hotels.

'Do you come here often?' Loveday wanted to know.

Charles gave her his charming smile. 'Never with such a delightful companion.' He might have added, And only because here I'm most unlikely to meet anyone I know. He wasn't doing any harm, he told himself. Loveday led a dull life; what could be kinder than to give her a taste of romance? And it would keep him amused for the next few weeks...

She was a dear little thing, he reflected as they drove back, but too quiet and dull for him. It amused him to see how she blossomed under his attention.

'We must do this again,' he told her. 'I'll be away next weekend, but there's a good film we might go to see one evening. Wednesday. I'll come for you about half past seven.'

'I'd like that, thank you,' she said. And, Loveday being Loveday, she added, 'I won't need to dress up? I haven't anything smart to wear.'

'No, no. You look very nice.'

He turned his head to smile at her. She was wearing something dull and unflattering, but the cinema he had in mind was well away from his usual haunts and he wasn't likely to see anyone who knew him.

He didn't get out of the car when they got back, but kissed her cheek and told her what a marvellous day it had been and then drove away before she had the key in the door. He had cut things rather fine; he had barely an hour in which to change for the evening.

Loveday climbed the stairs to the flat, to be met by an impatient Sam. She fed him and made a pot of tea before sitting down to drink it while she told him about her day. 'He's so nice,' she told Sam. 'He makes me laugh, and he makes me feel pretty and amusing although I know I'm not. We're going out again on Wednesday evening and I wish I had some pretty clothes to wear. He said it doesn't matter but I'd like to look my best for him. He notices what I'm wearing.' She sighed. 'Dr Fforde doesn't even see me—not as a girl, that is, only as his receptionist. And why I should think of him, I don't know.'

She was wrong, of course. Dr Fforde, coming to his rooms on Monday morning, at once saw the inner glow in Loveday's face and the sparkle in her eyes.

CHAPTER THREE

THE doctor bade her good morning and paused long enough to ask her if she had had a good weekend. 'You have friends to visit?' he wanted to know.

'Me? No. I hadn't time to make friends when I was with Miss Cattell,' she told him cheerfully.

So who or what had given her ordinary face that happy look? He went into his consulting room, thinking about it. It would hardly do for him to ask her how she spent her spare time, although he had a strong inclination to know that. Besides, it would be difficult to ask because her manner towards him had a distinct tinge of reserve. Probably she thought him too elderly to have an interest in her private life. A man approaching forty must seem middle-aged to a girl in her twenties.

He sat down to open his post and glanced up briefly when she came in with his coffee. The happy look was still there…

It seemed to Loveday that Wednesday took a long time in coming, and when it did she was in a fever of impatience; the last patient of the afternoon was elderly, nervous and inclined to want her own way, demanding a good deal of attention from the nurse and then sitting down again to repeat her symptoms once again to a patient Dr Fforde.

It was long after five when Loveday ushered her out, and it was almost an hour later when the nurse and Dr Fforde had gone too and she was at last ready to leave herself.

47

She sped up to the flat, fed an impatient Sam, made tea for herself and gobbled a sandwich left over from her lunch. She was hungry, but that was a small price to pay for an evening with Charles. She showered, changed into the jacket, skirt and a cream silk blouse, did her face with unusual care, brushed her mousy hair smooth and decided against her only hat. At least her shoes and handbag were good, even if they were no longer new.

She glanced out of the window; he would be here at any moment and he had been impatient on Sunday. She gave Sam a hug, locked up and hurried down to the street. She was just in time as Charles drew up.

He leaned over and opened the car door. 'There you are, darling. How clever of you to know that I hate being kept waiting.' When she had settled into the seat beside him he dropped a careless kiss on her cheek. She really was quite a taking little thing; it was a pity she dressed in such a dull fashion.

The film was just released, a triumph of modern cinema and Loveday, who hadn't been to the cinema for a long time, enjoyed it. When it ended and they had reached his car her heart lifted when he said, 'A drink and something to eat? It's still early.'

Eleven o'clock at night was late for her, now that she no longer had to keep the erratic hours Miss Cattell's household were obliged to put up with, and she had been going to her bed well before eleven. But she cast good sense to the winds and agreed.

To be disappointed. She was hungry, but Charles, it seemed, had dined earlier that evening, so 'drinks' were indifferent coffee and a bowl of nuts and tiny cheese biscuits in the bar of a nearby hotel. Not the usual hotel Charles frequented, and he made no attempt to dally over them. Loveday could see that he was anxious to be gone, and since she was by now as attracted to him as he had intended, she declared that she should go back to the flat.

'It's been a lovely evening,' she told him, 'and thank you for taking me.'

'My dearest girl, the pleasure was all mine.' He stopped before the consulting rooms, leaned across to open her door and then put an arm around her to kiss her. A sweet little thing, he reflected, but he was becoming the littlest bit bored with her. All the same he said, 'We must have another day out soon.'

He drove off, leaving her on the pavement. Loveday, unlocking the door, told herself that he must have had an urgent reason to rush away like that, and drowned the thought in the prospect of another day out with him.

'I have never been so happy,' she told Sam, eating her late supper of scrambled eggs on toast. And she was sure that she was. A nameless, niggling doubt at the back of her mind was easily lost in the remembrance of his kiss.

She made a mistake in the case notes in the morning, and forgot to give Dr Fforde a message from the hospital. Not an urgent one, but all the same there had been no excuse for forgetting it—except that she had been thinking of Charles.

The doctor accepted her apology with a nod and said nothing, but back in his home that evening he sat for a long time thinking about it.

Loveday was very careful during the next few days not to make any more mistakes. Never mind her vague dreams of a blissful future; the present was reality—security, a roof over her head, money in her pocket. Her scrupulous attention to her duties and her anxiety to please the doctor he found at first amusing, then puzzling. He didn't pretend to himself that he wasn't interested in her, but he was a man of no conceit and found it unlikley that a girl of her age, even if she was as level-headed as Loveday was, would wish to make a friend of a man so much older than she. He could only hope that whoever it was who had brought that look into her face would make her happy.

Charles phoned one morning during the week. Loveday had the place ready, the coffee set for the doctor and everything prepared for the day's work.

'Darling,' said Charles over the phone, 'I thought we might have a lovely evening on Saturday. Wear a pretty dress; we'll dine and dance.'

He hung up before she could reply.

It seemed that Saturday would never come. When it did she got up early and went down to the consulting rooms; she set everything to rights ready for Monday before hurrying to get a bus which would take her to Oxford Street.

She had raided her nest egg, shutting her eyes to the fact that she was making a great hole in her secure future, but no one—no man—had ever asked her out to dine and dance before, and certainly not a man such as Charles, so full of fun and so obviously liking her a lot, perhaps even loving her...

It took her an hour or two to find what she wanted; a plain sheath of a dress, and well cut, although the material from which it was made was cheap—but the colour was right: a pale bronze which gave her hair colour and flattered her eyes. There was also money enough for shoes, found after much searching on a bargain rail in a cheap shoe shop. They weren't leather, though they looked as though they were, and they went well with the dress.

She hurried back home with her purchases to give Sam his tea before she boiled an egg and made a pot of tea for herself. Then she began to get ready for the evening. It was a pity that Charles hadn't said at what time he would call for her...

She was ready far too soon, and sat peering out of the window into the street below. Perhaps he had forgotten…

It was almost eight o'clock when she saw his car stop before the house, and Loveday, being Loveday, with no thought of keeping him waiting or playing hard to get, flew down to the door.

He was sitting in the car, waiting for her, and because she was living for the moment in a delightful dream world of her own his casual manners were unnoticed. She got into the car beside him and he put an arm round her and kissed her lightly.

'Got that pretty dress?' he wanted to know, and looked doubtfully at her coat; it was plain and serviceable and obviously not in the height of fashion.

'Yes.' She smiled at him. 'I bought it this morning.'

He had planned the evening carefully: dinner at a small restaurant in Chelsea—smart enough to impress her but hardly likely to entertain anyone he might know—and afterwards there was a dance hall not too far away. It was hardly a place he would consider taking any of his acquaintances, but he suspected that to Loveday it would be the highlight of their evening.

Their table was in the corner of the restaurant, a pleasant enough place, with shaded lights and its dozen or so tables already filled. The food was good too, and he ordered champagne. She could have sat there for ever opposite him, listening to his amusing talk, smiling happily at his admiring glances, but they didn't linger over dinner.

'I'm longing to dance with you,' Charles told her.

The dance floor was crowded and very noisy, and hemmed in by other dancers, they scarcely moved. For that Loveday was secretly thankful, as her opportunities to go dancing had been non-existent at Miss Cattell's home. She was disappointed but not surprised when he declared impatiently that dancing was quite out of the question.

'A pity,' he told her as they left the place. 'Having to cut short a delightful evening.'

There would be other evenings, thought Loveday, and waited for him to say so, only he didn't. Indeed, he didn't mention seeing her again as he drove her back. He was unusually silent, and once or twice she thought that he was on the point of telling her something.

'Is there anything the matter?' she asked.

'Matter? What on earth put that idea into your head?' He sounded angry, but then a moment later said, 'Sorry, darling, I didn't mean to snap. I wanted this evening to be something special.'

He stopped outside the consulting rooms and turned to look at her. 'You wouldn't like to ask me up?'

'No, I wouldn't.' She smiled at him, and he put an arm round her shoulders and kissed her, then leaned forward to open her door.

She got out and turned to look at him. 'It was a lovely evening, Charles, thank you.' She waited for him to say something as she closed the door. But all he did was lift a hand in farewell and drive off. She stood on the pavement for a moment, disappointed that he hadn't said when they would meet again, and vaguely disturbed about it, but the memory of his kiss blotted uneasiness away. She unlocked the door and let herself into the house.

Dr Fforde, wanting some notes he had left in his consulting room, had walked round from his house, found them, put out his desk light, and was on his way through the waiting room when the sound of a car outside sent him to the window. He stood there, watching Loveday get out of the car, Charles drive away and her stillness before she turned to go into the house. He went then to open the door and switch on the landing light.

'Loveday.' His voice was reassuringly normal. 'I came to collect some notes I needed. 'I'm on my way out.'

He came down the stairs, switching on lights as he came, and found her standing in the hall.

'I've been out,' said Loveday unnecessarily, and added for good measure, 'With Charles.'

'Yes, I saw you and the car from the window. You've had a pleasant evening?'

She smiled at him. She would have liked to have told him all about her and Charles. He was, she reflected, the kind of person you wanted to tell things to. Instead she said happily, 'Oh, I had a lovely time,' and then, because she wanted to make it all quite clear, 'Charles has taken me out several times—we—seem to get on well together.'

Dr Fforde put his hand on the door. He smiled, but all he said was, 'Sleep well!'

In the flat, she told Sam all about it. 'I'm not sure if Dr Fforde likes me going out with Charles. He's too nice to say so…'

She hung the pretty dress away and wondered when she would wear it again. Soon, she hoped.

She was used to being lonely. Sunday passed happily enough, with attending church and a walk, then back to Sam's company and the Sunday papers. Monday couldn't come quickly enough—there was sure to be a phone call from Charles. She counted her money once again. Perhaps a long skirt and a pretty top would be an asset? Something she could wear which wasn't too noticeable? They would probably go dancing again, somewhere quieter—the dance hall hadn't been the kind of place Charles would normally visit, she thought, but of course it had been near the restaurant.

Her spirits dwindled with the passing days. She went about her work quietly, careful not to make mistakes, passed the time of day with Nurse, answered the doctor when he spoke to her in her usual quiet way, but by the end of the week the happiness he had seen in her face was subdued.

It was on Thursday evening after the last patient had gone that he called her into his consulting rooms.

He was standing by the window looking down into the street below. He said over his shoulder. 'Loveday, there is something you should know…'

Miss Priss was coming back! She swallowed a sudden rush of feelings and said politely, 'Yes, Doctor?'

He turned to look at her. He said in a harsh voice, 'Charles is to be married in two weeks…his fiancée has been in America. You are unaware of this?'

She nodded, and then said, 'If you don't mind, I'd like to go to the flat. I'll clear up later.' Her voice didn't sound quite like hers, but it was almost steady. On no account must she burst into tears or scream that she didn't believe him. Dr Fforde wasn't a man to tell lies—lies to turn her world upside down.

He didn't speak, but opened the door for her. And when she looked up at him and whispered, 'Thank you,' from a pale face, the kindness of his smile almost overset her.

She let herself into the flat and, almost unaware of what she was doing, fed Sam, made tea and sat down to drink it. This was a nightmare from which she would presently wake, she told herself. She was still sitting there, the tea cold in front of her, Sam looking anxious on her lap, when the flat door opened and Dr Fforde came in.

'I have a key,' he observed. 'I think you will feel better if you talk about it.' He glanced at the tea. 'We will have tea together and while we drink it we can discuss the matter.'

He put the kettle on and made fresh tea, found clean cups and saucers and put a nicely laid tray on the table between them. Loveday, watching him wordlessly, felt surprise at the ease with which he performed the small household duty.

He poured the tea and put a cup in front of her. 'Tell me about it—Charles has been taking you out? You began to feel that he was falling in love with you?' He added, 'Drink your tea.'

She sipped obediently. There was no reason why she should answer him, for this was her own business, none of his, and yet she heard herself say meekly, 'Not very often. Once or twice to the cinema and a day in the country and last Saturday evening.' She said in a voice thick with tears, 'I've been a silly fool, haven't I?'

'No,' he said gently. 'How were you to know if Charles didn't tell you? I don't suppose he deliberately set out to hurt you. He has fallen in and out of love many times, but he is to marry a strong-minded American girl who will make sure that he loves only her. He was having a last fling. He has been selfish and uncaring and has probably already forgotten you. That sounds harsh, but the obvious thing is to forget him, too. Believe me, you will, even though at the moment you don't believe me.'

Loveday wiped her hands across her wet eyes like a child. 'How could I have been so stupid? You have only to look at me. I'm not even a little bit pretty and I wear all the wrong clothes.' She suddenly began to cry again. 'I bought that dress just for the evening because he said I ought to wear pretty colours!' She gulped and sniffed. 'Please will you go away now?'

'No. Go and wash your face and do your hair and get

a coat. We will have our supper together.' He glanced at his watch. 'Mrs Duckett, my housekeeper, will have it ready in half an hour or so. You will eat everything put before you and then I shall bring you back here and you will go straight to bed and sleep. In the morning your heart will be sore, and perhaps a little cracked, but not broken.'

He sounded so kind that she wanted to weep again. 'I'm not hungry...' But all the same she went to the bedroom and did her hair, and the best she could with her poor pink-nosed face and puffy eyelids. Presently she went back to where he was waiting, the tea things tidied away and Sam on his knee.

She hadn't expected the house in the mews, a rather larger one than its neighbours, with windows on either side of its front door flanked by little bay trees. He ushered her into the narrow hall and Mrs Duckett came to meet them.

'This is my receptionist, Miss Loveday West,' said the doctor. 'She has had an upsetting experience and it seemed to me that one of your splendid suppers would make her feel better, Mrs Duckett. Loveday, this is my housekeeper, Mrs Duckett.'

Loveday shook hands and the housekeeper gave her a motherly look. Been crying her eyes out, by the look of it, she reflected, and took the coat the doctor had taken from Loveday.

'Ten minutes or so.' She beamed at them both. 'Just nice time for a drop of sherry.'

The doctor opened the door and pushed Loveday gently ahead of him. The room had a window at each end and there was a cheerful fire burning in the elegant fireplace between them. It was a charming room, with sofas on each side of the hearth, a Pembroke table between them and several bookshelves crowded with books. There was a long-case clock in one corner, and the whole room was lighted by shaded lamps on the various small tables.

'Come by the fire,' said the doctor. 'Do you like dogs?'

When she nodded she saw two beady eyes peering from a shock of hair, watching her from a basket by a winged armchair by the window.

'A dog—he's yours?'

'Yes. He stays in his basket because he's been hurt.' Dr Fforde bent to stroke the tousled head. 'He got knocked down in the street and no one owns him.'

'You'll keep him?'

'Why not? He's a splendid fellow and will be perfectly fit in a week or so.' He had poured sherry and offered her a glass. 'He has two broken legs. They're in plaster.'

'May I stroke him?'

'Of course. I don't think he's had much kindness in his life so far.'

Loveday knelt by the basket and offered a hand, and then gently ran it over the dog's rough coat. 'He's lovely. What do you call him?'

'Can you think of a suitable name? I have had him only a couple of days.'

She thought about it, aware that beneath this fragile conversation about the dog there was hidden a great well of unhappiness which at any minute threatened to overflow.

'Something that sounds friendly—you know, like a family dog with a lot of children.' She paused, thinking that sounded like nonsense. 'Bob or Bertie or Rob.'

'We will call him Bob. Come and finish your sherry and we'll have our supper.'

She wished Bob goodbye, and he stuck out a pink tongue and licked the back of her hand. 'Oh, I do hope he'll get well quickly,' said Loveday.

She had expected supper to be a light evening meal, but

it wasn't supper at all. It was dinner at its best, eaten in a small dining room, sitting on Hepplewhite chairs at a table covered with a damask cloth and set with silver and glass. There was soup from a Coalport soup plate, chicken, cooked deliciously in a wine sauce, potato purée and tiny sprouts, and one of Mrs Duckett's sherry trifles to follow.

The doctor poured a crisp white wine and maintained a steady flow of undemanding talk, giving her no chance to think about anything other than polite answers. They had coffee at the table before he drove her back to the consulting rooms, went up to the flat with her, switched on the lights, wished Sam an affable goodnight and went back down the stairs after bidding her a quiet goodnight. She tried to stammer out her thanks but he waved them aside.

'I'll see you in the morning, Loveday,' he told her. 'Go to bed and go to sleep.'

And, strangely enough, that was what she did. She woke early, though, and her unhappiness, held at bay the evening before, took over. But now, in the light of the morning, she was able to think about it with a degree of good sense. She saw now that she had behaved like a lovesick teenager—just the kind of silly girl Charles had needed to keep him amused while his future wife was away.

That didn't make her unhappiness any the less. She had her dreams and she had been carried away by what she had supposed was Charles's delight in her company. She told herself that it was because she had been so little in a man's company that she had mistaken his attentions for real feeling. This was a sensible conclusion, which none the less didn't stop her crying her eyes out, so that she had to spend a long time doing things to her face before she went down to the consulting rooms.

She thought she had made rather a good job of it as she studied her face in the large mirror between the windows in the waiting room, but it was a good thing that she couldn't read the doctor's thoughts as he came in.

He noted the puffed eyelids and the still pink nose and the resolutely smiling mouth and reflected that she had one of the most unassuming faces he had ever seen. Except for those glorious eyes, of course. So what was it about her that took so much of his interest? An interest which he had felt the first time he had met her...

He went to his consulting room, accepted the coffee she brought him, and considered the matter. He was in love with her, of course; it was not a passing fancy. He had over the years considered marrying, and had, like any other man, fancied himself in love from time to time. But he had always known that the girl in question hadn't been the right one, that sooner or later he would meet a woman whom he would love and want to have for his wife. But now was hardly the time to tell Loveday that. Patience was called for, and he had plenty of that.

He had a busy day ahead of him, and would be spending the greater part of it at the hospital, so beyond giving Loveday instructions about patients and the time of his return, he had nothing to say. He could see that she was determined to keep her feelings concealed.

Only that evening, as he left to go home, he paused at her desk, where she was still busy.

'Bob spent half an hour in the garden this morning. You would be surprised at what he can manage to do on two legs and with a lot of help.'

She said gravely, 'He is a darling dog. I think he will be devoted to you; you saved his life.'

He smiled down at her. 'I think he will be a fine fellow once he is well again. Goodnight, Loveday.'

It was quiet after he had gone. It would be absurd, she told herself, to say that she missed him. She finished the tidying up and went upstairs to Sam's welcoming voice. She had got through the day, hadn't she? she reflected, and if she could get through one day she could get through as many more as she must before she could finally forget Charles.

The following week seemed endless; she listened to Nurse's confidences concerning her boyfriend with sympathy, presented a welcoming face to the doctor's patients, and carried on long one-sided conversations with Sam.

She planned her weekend with him. 'I shall go shopping on Saturday afternoon,' she told him, 'and on Sunday I'll go to church in the morning and then to Hyde Park in the afternoon, and we'll have a cosy evening together.'

And Sam, grown comfortably stout and placid, got onto her lap and went to sleep. Life for him, at any rate, was quite perfect.

The last of Friday afternoon's patients came late. Nurse was annoyed because that meant she couldn't leave punctually, and just before the patient was ushered out the phone rang. Five minutes later Dr Fforde left too.

He bade the nurse goodnight, told Loveday to lock up and that he would be at the hospital, and went away.

Nurse followed him almost at once, grumbling because she would have to rush home and change before going out for the evening. 'And I wanted to get my hair done,' she complained, slamming the door behind her.

Which left Loveday alone, putting things to rights. She would be down in the morning to make sure that everything was ready for Monday, but all the same she liked to leave the place just so. She didn't hurry for she had no reason to do so, and even though after a week her unhappiness was dulled, her solitary evenings were the most difficult part of the day.

She spent longer than she needed in the consulting rooms the next morning, keeping her mind resolutely on prosaic things such as her shopping list and Monday's patients. The phone rang several times too—patients wanting to make appointments—and just as she was about to lock up, Mrs Seward rang.

'I know Fforde isn't there,' she told Loveday, 'but would you leave a message for him? Ask him to come and see me on Monday if he can manage it? If he knows before his morning patients he may be able to arrange something. Thank you. Am I talking to the girl with the green eyes?'

'Yes.'

'Miss Priss not back yet? I'm sure you're filling her shoes very competently. You won't forget the message?'

She rang off and Loveday thought what a pleasant, friendly voice she had. Perhaps the doctor was going to marry her...

She was on the way upstairs to her flat when she heard the front door bang shut. It wouldn't be Todd, he used the entrance at the back of the house, and the three other medical men who had rooms there were all out of London for the weekend, Todd had told her that before he had gone home the previous evening.

Not quite frightened, but cautious, Loveday started down the stairs.

Dr Fforde was coming up them, two at a time. He stood on the landing, looking up at her.

'I'm glad I find you in,' he observed. 'Can you spare an hour later on today? Late afternoon, perhaps? I'll call for you around four o'clock. Bob is doing splendidly, but I fancy he needs some distraction—a new face. Will you come?'

'Well, if you think it might help him to get better quickly... He can't go out?'

'Into the garden. With two of us he might feel encouraged to hobble around in his plasters. He has forgotten how to enjoy life. Indeed, I think that he never had that opportunity.'

'Oh, the poor dog. Of course I'll come.'

'Good!' He was already going back downstairs. 'I'll see you later.'

'Oh, wait!' cried Loveday. 'I almost forgot. Mrs Seward phoned. She asked if you would arrange to see her on Monday; she wanted you to know as soon as possible when you got here on Monday morning.'

He nodded, said, 'Thanks,' and went on his way out of the house.

There would be no time to sit and brood; Loveday fed Sam, had a quick lunch, and hurried to the shops. They knew her there by now, with her modest purchases of lamb chops and sausages, tins of cat food, butter, tea and coffee, some greengrocery and a loaf and, last of all, another book or two. A nice, quiet little lady they told each other, and occasionally they popped something extra into her basket.

She went back in good time to do her hair and her face, and leave the ever-hungry Sam something to eat on his saucer, before going to the window to watch for the doctor's car. When it came, instead of waiting there for her to go down, he got out and came into the house and all the way to her flat to knock on her door.

She couldn't help but compare his easy good manners with Charles's careless ones, and a small shaft of pleasure shot through her as he ushered her into the car and closed the door.

Bob was pleased to see her, and instead of lying rather listlessly in his basket he made valiant efforts to sit up.

'Oh, you clever boy,' said Loveday. 'You're better! He is better?' she asked anxiously.

'Yes. The vet's pleased with him. It wasn't only the legs, he was in poor shape, but now he's getting his strength back. We'll go into the garden for a few minutes and you can see what he can do.'

The doctor carried the little dog outside and set him down gently, and after a few moments Bob dragged himself onto his two front legs. He wasn't sure what to do with the ungainly plastered back legs, but presently he stood, a bit wobbly, looking pleased with himself.

'Once he's discovered that he can use his legs without pain, even if they're clumsy, there'll be no holding him.' The doctor picked him up and carried him back indoors and settled Loveday in a chair by the fire.

'Shall we have tea? Bob loves company.'

Mrs Duckett's teas were like no other: there were muffins in a silver dish, tiny sandwiches, fairy cakes, and a cake thick with fruit and nuts. It was just the right meal for a chilly autumn day, sitting round the fire, talking of this and that, both of them perfectly at ease.

Dr Fforde, who was skilled in the art of extracting information from patients who were reluctant to give it, went to work on Loveday.

'No family?' he enquired casually. 'Surely someone— an aunt or uncle or cousin—even if you have little to do with them?'

He was an easy man to talk to. 'I was brought up by an aunt; she died some years ago. There's another aunt—my father's much older sister. She lives in a village on the edge of Dartmoor. We send each other cards at Christmas but I've never met her. I—I haven't liked to ask her if I might go and see her. I expect she thinks I have a satisfactory life here, and it's a long way. In any case, Miss Cattell didn't like me having a holiday. I hated being there, but it was a job, and I'm not trained for anything, am I?'

He agreed in a non-committal way. 'I have no doubt that you would have no difficulty in getting work. There is always a shortage of good receptionists. But you would like to visit your aunt?'

'Yes. Well, I mean, she is family, isn't she? If you see what I mean? But I expect she's happy living in Devon and would hate to have her life disrupted, even for a brief visit.' She added, 'And I'm very happy here.'

He was looking at her so thoughtfully that she hurried to change the subject. 'This is a charming house. You must like coming home each day.'

'Indeed I do, but I'm fond of the country too. I don't know Dartmoor at all; it must be very different...'

The casualness of his remark encouraged her to say, 'Oh, I'm sure it is. My aunt lives in a small village, somewhere near Ashburton. Buckland-in-the-Moor. It sounds lovely, but I expect it's lonely. It's a long way away.'

The doctor, having obtained all the information he wanted, began to talk of Bob and his future, which led naturally enough to Sam, his intelligence, his appetite and his delightful company...

Loveday glanced at the clock. 'Heavens, it's almost six o'clock. If you don't mind, I'd like to go back to the flat. It's been lovely, but I've several things to do and the evenings go so quickly.'

Which wasn't true. They dragged from one hour to the next while she did her best to forget Charles's red car screaming to a halt below her window...

The doctor made no demur. She bade Bob goodbye, thanked the doctor for her tea and got back into the car. At the consulting rooms she began to say, 'You don't need to get out—'

She could have saved her breath; he went upstairs with her, opened the flat door and switched on the lights, and bade Sam a cheerful good evening before expressing, in the briefest manner, his thanks for her company.

'Bob was delighted to see you,' he assured her. He had been delighted too, but he wasn't going to say so.

Loveday, listening to his footsteps receding on the stairs, was aware of a loneliness worse than usual. 'It's because he's such a large man that I notice when he's not here,' she told Sam.

CHAPTER FOUR

IT WAS on Monday morning that she saw the doctor had given himself a day off on Wednesday. She guessed why at once. It would be Charles's wedding day—a guess confirmed presently when Nurse came. She had a glossy magazine under one arm.

'Look at this.' She found the page and handed it to Loveday. 'Remember Dr Fforde's young cousin, who came here a few weeks ago? He's getting married—here's his picture and that's his fiancée. Pretty, isn't she? They are going to live in America, lucky them. The wedding is on Wednesday—a big one—you know, huge hats and white satin and bridesmaids. I must say they make a handsome pair.'

She took the magazine back again. 'Dr Fforde will go— he's bound to, isn't he? They're cousins, even if he is a lot older.'

'She's very pretty,' said Loveday, and wished that the phone would ring so that she had an excuse not to stand there gossiping. And the phone did ring, so that Nurse went away to the dressing room which was her workplace. Since there was a busy day ahead of them there would be little chance of more chatting. Loveday heaved a sigh of relief and turned a welcoming smile onto the first patient.

But, busy or not, it was hard not to keep thinking of Charles. She knew now that the whole thing had been nothing but an amusing interlude to him, and if she hadn't led such a narrow life she would have recognised that and treated the whole affair in the same light-hearted manner. But knowing that didn't make it any easier to forget…

On Tuesday the doctor was at the hospital all day, returning at five o'clock to see two patients in his consulting rooms. It had been very quiet all day, although Loveday had been kept busy enough making appointments. It had been a good opportunity to sort through the papers scattered on the doctor's desk, tidy them into heaps and write one or two reminder notes for him. Tomorrow he would be away all day, but since he had said nothing she supposed that she would be there as usual, taking calls and messages.

Neither patient stayed long, and it was barely six o'clock when she ushered the last one out and began to tidy up.

The doctor left soon after, but first he stopped to tell her that he had switched on the answering-machine. 'Anything urgent will be referred to Dr Gregg,' he told her, 'and you need only be here between ten o'clock and noon, then again between five o'clock and six. I'll be in as usual on Thursday.' He smiled suddenly. 'Would you do something for me? Would you go to my house in the early afternoon and give Bob half an hour in the garden? Mrs Duckett is nervous of hurting him. He's managing very well now, but he does need someone there.' He added, 'That is, unless you have planned something?'

'No, no. I haven't. Of course I'll go and keep Bob company for a little while. Mrs Duckett won't mind?'

'Mrs Duckett will be delighted. Goodnight, Loveday.'

She would do her weekly shopping in the morning, Loveday decided, and go to the doctor's house around two o'clock. She sat down to make out her small list of groceries. 'And a tin of sardines for you,' she promised Sam.

* * *

The doctor's house was a brisk ten minutes' walk away.
Loveday knocked on its elegant front door just after two
o'clock and was admitted by a smiling Mrs Duckett.

'Bob's waiting for you. I told him you'd be here soon.
He misses the doctor when he's not home. I'm fond of
him, but I'm a bit nervous on account of his legs. Keep
your coat on, miss, it'll be chilly in the garden. Half an
hour, the doctor said, and then you're to have a cup of tea
before you go.'

She bustled Loveday into the sitting room. 'Look at that,
then. He's trying to get onto his legs he's that happy to
see you.'

She opened the doors onto the garden and trotted away
with the reminder that tea would be brought at three
o'clock.

Loveday knelt and put an arm round Bob's shoulders.
Now that he was fed and rested and belonged to someone
he was quite handsome, although his looks could be at-
tributed to a variety of ancestors. Not that that mattered in
the least, she assured him.

She picked him up and took him into the garden, and
once there he took heart and struggled around, dragging
his cumbersome plastered legs, obviously glad of her company. After a time they went back to the house and sat
companionably side by side, he in his basket, Loveday on
the floor beside him. He was a splendid companion too,
listening with every sign of interest while she told him
about Charles getting married and how lucky he was to
have such a kind master, and presently Mrs Duckett came
with the tea tray. There was dainty china and a little silver
teapot, crumpets in a covered dish, little cakes and wafer-
thin bread and butter, and, of course, a biscuit for Bob.

Loveday enjoyed every morsel and strangely enough she

didn't think about the wedding, only that tea would have been even nicer if the doctor had been there with them.

She left soon after and hurried back to the consulting rooms, then sat at her desk from five o'clock until the clock struck six, answering a few calls on the phone and making sure that everything was ready for the morning.

The doctor arrived punctually the next morning, and paused on his way to thank her for visiting Bob, but if she had hoped for him to mention the wedding she was to be disappointed. With the remark that they had a busy morning before them, he went into his consulting room and closed the door.

Watching Sam scoff his supper that evening, she wondered aloud if she would be asked on Friday morning to visit Bob at the weekend, but here again she was to be disappointed; beyond reminding her that he would be at the hospital on Monday morning and wishing her a pleasant weekend he had nothing to say.

'And why I should have expected anything else I have no idea,' said Loveday, expressing her thoughts, as usual, to Sam.

The weather had changed, becoming dull and wet and windy. All the same, she wrapped up warmly and went walking. Not to the shops; she might spend too much money if she did that, and the nest egg in the Post Office was growing steadily. It would have been even larger if she hadn't bought that dress...

She was beginning to feel secure; there had been no news of Miss Priss, and the weeks were mounting up. Her return had receded into a vague worry which was becoming vaguer every day.

She was in the consulting rooms in good time on Monday morning, for although the doctor might not be there there was plenty to do. She sorted the post and laid it ready on his desk, noting with a small sigh of relief that there was no envelope with Miss Priss's spiky writing on it.

That letter was in the doctor's pocket, for it had been sent to his house. He had read it and then read it again; Miss Priss's mother had died and she would be glad to return to work as soon as she had settled her affairs.

I shall give up our home. It is a rented house and I do not wish to remain here. Would you consider allowing me to live in the flat on the top floor of the consulting rooms? I would be happy to receive a reduced salary in this case, or pay rent. I have no family and few friends here and must find somewhere to live. I would not have suggested this, but I have worked for you for so many years that I feel I can venture to give voice to this possible arrangement.

Of course he would agree to it; Miss Priss was a trusted right hand, had been for years, and the arrangement would give her a secure future and a home. She must be in her fifties, he thought, at a time in life when the years ahead should offer that security. A letter, reassuring her, must be written, and Loveday must be told.

The answer to Loveday, as far as he was concerned, was to marry her. But first he must allow her to get over Charles and, that done, he would wait until the cracks in her heart were healed. But in the meantime she would need a roof over her head...

He wrote reassuringly to Miss Priss: she was to have the flat and to resume her duties just as soon as she felt able. He suggested two weeks ahead. He would be delighted to have her back and she was to regard the flat as her home until such time as she might wish to leave.

The letter written, he turned his thoughts to Loveday. Before he told her, he decided, he would drive down to the remote village where her aunt lived.

The orderly days slid by and it seemed to him that Loveday was beginning to forget Charles. She was quiet, but then she always was; however, her face in repose was no longer sad.

Early on Saturday morning he started on the long drive to the village on Dartmoor with Bob propped up beside him. It would probably be a wild-goose chase but it was the obvious thing to do...

It was a journey of about two hundred miles, but once free of London and its sprawling suburbs the road was fairly empty, and the further west he went the emptier it became. On a quiet stretch of road he stopped for coffee and to see to Bob's needs, and then he drove on until he reached the bypass to Exeter and took the road to the moor. Presently he turned off and drove through Ashburton and into the empty country beyond. It was a clear late-autumn day and the majestic sweep of the moorland hills swept away from him into the distance. The road was narrow now, and sheep roamed to and fro between the craggy rocks. Bob, who had never seen a sheep, was entranced.

The village, when he reached it, was charming, built on the banks of the river Dart and surrounded by trees. It had a handful of grey stone houses and an ancient church, a cheerful-looking pub and one or two bigger houses near the church. The doctor stopped at the pub and went inside.

The bar was small and cosy, with a bright log fire burning and comfortable chairs set beside the tables. It would be a focal point in the village, he reflected, and a cheerful haven on a bleak winter's evening.

Of course he could have lunch, said the elderly man behind the bar. A pasty and a pint of the best ale in the country, and the dog was welcome to come in.

Bob, carried in and sat gently on the floor, caused quite a stir. The two young men playing darts abandoned their game to come and look at his plastered legs and an old man by the fire declared that he'd never seen anything like it before. Their interest in him engendered a friendly atmosphere and a still deeper interest when the doctor mentioned that he had driven down from London.

'Lost, are you?' one of the young men wanted to know.

'No, no. I've come to visit someone living here. A Miss West?'

'Up at Bates Cottage?' volunteered the landlord, setting down the pasty and a bowl of water for Bob. 'Know her, do you, sir? Elderly, like, and not given to visitors?'

He looked at the doctor with frank curiosity.

'I have never met her. I have come to see her on behalf of her niece.'

'Oh, aye, she's got a niece—sends her a card at Christmas. Me ma cleans for her and sees to her post and shopping. She told Miss West she should have her niece to stay, but the old lady's independent, like, don't want to be a nuisance.'

'I should like to go and see her this afternoon...'

'As good a time as any. It's the last house at the end of the lane past the church. Too big for her, but she won't move. Got her dogs and cats and birds.'

'Could you put me up for the night?' asked the doctor.

'That I can,' said the landlord. 'And you could do with a nice bit of supper, no doubt?'

'Indeed I could. I'll go and call on Miss West before it gets dark.' He paid his bill, ordered pints all round, picked up Bob and went back to the car. It was no distance to

Miss West's house, but unless she invited Bob in he would have to stay in the car.

The house was built of grey stone and thatched, and it was a good deal larger than the other cottages in the village. The curtains were undrawn and in the beginnings of an early dusk the lamplight from the room beside the stout front door shone cheerfully.

He went up the path and tugged the old-fashioned bell. The elderly lady who opened it was small and brisk.

'I'm Miss West. Are you looking for me? If so why? I don't know you.'

The doctor perceived that he would need his bedside manner.

'I apologise for calling upon you in this manner, but first I must ask you if you are indeed the aunt of Loveday West?'

She stood staring at him. 'Yes, I am. Come inside.' She peered past him. 'What is that in your car?'

'My dog.'

'Fetch him.'

'He has two legs in plaster and is somewhat of an invalid.'

'All the more reason to bring him inside.'

When he'd fetched Bob she led the way from the narrow hall to the sitting room, which was nicely lighted, warmed by a brisk open fire and comfortably furnished.

'While you are explaining why you have come to see me we may as well have tea. Sit there, near the fire—your dog can sit on the rug.'

The doctor did as he was told. 'His name is Bob.'

Now that he was in the lighted room he could see her clearly. She was in her late sixties or early seventies, he judged, and what she lacked in height she made up for by the strength of her personality. A lady to be reckoned with, he reflected, feeling a little amused, with her plain face, fierce dark eyes and iron-grey hair tugged back into an old-fashioned bun at the back of her head.

He sat down with Bob's head on his feet. He had liked the old lady on sight, but wondered if he was making a mistake. He would know that when he had told her about Loveday.

He got up and took the tea tray from her as she came back into the room. He set it on a small table, then waited until she had sat down before resuming his seat. Good manners came to him as naturally as breathing. Miss West, pouring the tea, liked him for that.

'If I might introduce myself?' suggested the doctor, accepting a cup of tea. 'Andrew Fforde—I'm a doctor. I have a practice in London and work at a London hospital.'

Miss West, sitting very upright in her chair, nodded. 'Give Bob a biscuit. Is he good with cats?'

'My housekeeper has a cat; they get on well together.'

'Then be good enough to open the kitchen door so that my cats and Tim can come in.'

He did as he was asked and three cats came into the sitting room. None of them in their first youth, they ignored Bob and sat down in a tidy row before the fire. Plodding along behind them was an odd dog, with a grey muzzle and a friendly eye, who breathed over Bob and sat down heavily on the doctor's feet.

Miss West passed him the cake dish. 'I have not seen Loveday since she was a very small girl. She wrote to me when her other aunt died. She made it plain that she was living in easy circumstances and has never asked for help of any kind. We exchange cards at Christmas. I have thought of her as one of these young women with a career and a wish to live their own lives without encumbrances of any sort.' She sipped her tea from a delicate china cup. 'Perhaps I have been mistaken?'

When he didn't answer, she said, 'Tell me what you have come to tell me.'

He put down his cup and saucer and told her. He added no embellishments and no opinions of his own, and when he had finished he added, 'It seemed to me right that you should know this…'

'Is she pretty?'

'No, I think perhaps one would call her rather plain. But she has a beauty which has nothing to do with looks. She has beautiful green eyes and soft mousy hair. She is small and she has a charming voice.'

'Fat? Thin?'

'Slim and nicely rounded.'

'You're in love with her?'

'Yes. I hope to marry her, but first she must recover from her meeting with Charles.'

Miss West stroked a cat which had climbed onto her lap. 'How old are you?'

'Thirty-eight. Loveday is twenty-four.'

'I like you, Dr Fforde. I don't like many people, and I have only just met you, nevertheless, I like you. Do whatever you think is the best for Loveday, and bring her here until she is ready to go with you as your wife.'

'That will be for her to decide,' he said quietly. 'But if she chooses to go her own way, then I shall make sure that she has a good job and a secure future.'

Miss West said, 'You love her as much as that?'

'Yes.' He smiled at her. 'Thank you for seeing me and giving me your willing help. May I let you know if our plans will be possible? It depends upon Loveday.'

'If Loveday decides to come and stay with me I shall make her welcome. And I wish you luck, Dr Fforde.'

'Thank you.' He would need it, he reflected on his way back to the pub. He had no right to interfere in Loveday's life and she would probably tell him so…

The small bar was full, and although he was stared at with frank curiosity, they were friendly stares.

The landlord, drawing him a pint, asked cheerfully if he had found Miss West. 'Nice old lady—lived here for a lifetime, she has. Don't hold with travel. There's a steak pie and our own sprouts for your supper, sir. Seven o'clock suit you? And if you let me know what your dog will eat…?' He eyed Bob, braced against the doctor's legs. 'Nice little beast. Seeing as he's an invalid, like, I'll put an old rug in your room for him.'

The doctor slept soundly. He had done what he had come to do, though whether it was the right thing only time would tell.

As for Bob, he was with his master and that was all that mattered to him. He had had a splendid supper and the old rug was reassuringly rich in smells: of wood ash and spilt food and ingrained dirt from boots. Just the thing to soothe a dog to sleep.

The doctor left after an unhurried breakfast, taking his time over the return trip to London. He had a lot to think about and he could do that undisturbed. He stopped for coffee and to accommodate Bob's needs and then, since the road was almost empty, he didn't stop again until he reached home.

Mrs Duckett spent Sunday afternoons with her sister and the house was quiet. But there was soup keeping warm on the Aga and cold meat and salad set out on the kitchen table. There was a note from Mrs Duckett telling him that she would cook him his dinner when she returned later.

He fed Bob and went to his study, to immerse himself in work. There was always plenty of paperwork; even with the secretary who came twice a week his desk was never empty. It wasn't until a faint aroma of something delicious caused him to twitch his splendid nose that he paused. Mrs Duckett was back and he was hungry.

Loveday went to bed early in her little flat, happily unaware of the future which was to be so soon disturbed.

The next day the doctor was due to go to the hospital after he had seen his patients at the consulting rooms, and he would be there for the rest of the day, but there was almost half an hour before he needed to leave. He went into the waiting room and found Loveday filing away patients' notes and writing up his daily diary ready for the morning.

She looked up as he went in. 'I'll type those two letters and leave them on your desk,' she told him. 'If there's anything urgent I could phone you at the hospital?'

'Yes, I'm booked up for the morning, aren't I? Use your discretion and fit in patients where you can. Anything really urgent, refer them to me at the hospital. I shall be there until six o'clock at least.'

He leaned against the desk, looking at her. 'I had a letter from Miss Priss. Her mother has died and she asks to come back to work in ten days' time; she also asks if she might have the flat in which to live. She has no family and her mother's house was rented.'

Loveday had gone a little pale. 'I'm so sorry Miss Priss's mother has died. But I'm glad that she has somewhere to come to where she can make her home. When would you like me to leave?'

'In a week's time? That gives me ample opportunity to ask around and find another similar job for you. I know a great many people and it shouldn't be too difficult.'

She said quickly, 'That is very kind of you, but I'm sure that I can find work…'

He said harshly, 'You will allow me to help you? I have no intention of allowing you to be homeless and workless. You came here to fill an emergency at my request; you will at least allow me to pay my debt.'

'Isn't a week rather a short time? I mean to find another job for me? Besides, you're busy all day…'

It was just the opening he had hoped for. 'Perhaps it may take longer than a week. You told me that you have an aunt living in Devon. Would you go and stay with her until I can get you fixed up?'

'But I've never seen her, at least not since I was a very little girl, and she might not want to have me to stay. And it's miles away…'

He said quietly, 'I went to see your aunt on Saturday, after I received Miss Priss's letter. You see, Loveday, I had to think of something quickly. She is quite elderly and I liked her—and she is both eager and willing for you to stay with her until you can get settled again.'

'You went all that way to see my aunt? Your weekend wasted…?'

'Not wasted, and, as I said, I like to pay my debts, Loveday.'

He straightened up and went to the door. 'Will you think about it and let me know in the morning? It's a sensible solution to the problem, you know.'

He smiled at her then, and went away. He wanted very much to stay and comfort her, to tell her that she had no need to worry, that he would look after her and love her. Instead he had told her everything in a matter-of-fact voice which gave away none of his feelings. The temptation to cajole her into accepting his offer was great, but he resisted it. He wanted her to love him—but only of her own free will.

Loveday sat very still; she felt as though someone had hit her very hard on the head and taken away her power to think. She had managed to answer the doctor sensibly, matching his own matter-of-fact manner, but now there was no need to do that. A week, she thought—seven days in which to find a job. She would have to start finding it at once, for of course there was no question of her accepting his offer of help.

She began to cry quietly. Not because she was once more with an undecided future but because that future would be without him. This calm, quiet man who had come to her rescue and who, she had no doubt, once he had made sure that she had another job, would dismiss her from his mind. She gave a great sniff, wiping the tears away with the back of her hand. After all, he had Mrs Seward, hadn't he?

Loveday, who had never felt jealous in her life before, was suddenly flooded with it.

Presently she stopped crying; it was a waste of time and was of no help at all. She put away the rest of the patients' notes, and then, since she would have the afternoon to get things ready for the next day, she selected the most likely newspapers and magazines to contain job advertisements and took herself off to the flat.

She explained it all to Sam, who yawned and went back to sleep, so she made a pot of tea, cut a sandwich and sat down to look through the job vacancy columns. There were plenty of vacancies—all of them for those with computer skills or, failing that, willing to undertake kitchen duties or work in launderettes. Since she had no knowledge of computers it would have to be something domestic. And why stay in London? Since she wouldn't see the doctor again, the further away she got from him the better.

'Out of sight, out of mind,' said Loveday, and because she was unhappy, and a little afraid of the future, she started to cry again.

But not for long. Presently she restored her face to its normal, or almost normal appearance and went back to the consulting room. She tidied up and got everything ready for the next day, made several appointments too, and brought the daily diary up to date, and when Mrs Seward phoned during the afternoon she answered her in a pleasant manner.

It was hard to dislike Mrs Seward; she was friendly and she had a nice voice. She sighed when Loveday told her that the doctor was at the hospital.

'I'll ring there and see if I can leave a message,' she told Loveday, 'but leave a note on his desk, will you? It's not urgent, but I do want to talk to him.'

Loveday went to bed early, since sitting alone in the flat while her thoughts tumbled around in her head was of no use, but her last waking thought was that nothing would persuade her to accept the doctor's suggestion.

When she sorted out the post in the morning there was a letter for her. From her aunt.

It was a long letter, written in a spidery hand, and, typically of Miss West, didn't beat about the bush. She had had a visit from Dr Fforde and agreed with him that the sensible thing to do was for Loveday to spend a few days with her while suitable work was found for her.

It is obvious that he is a man who has influence and moreover feels that he is indebted to you, as indeed he is. We know nothing of each other, but I shall be glad of your company. We are, after all, family. I live very

*quietly, but from what I hear from Dr Fforde you are
not one of these modern career girls. I look forward to
seeing you.*

There was a PS: *Bring your cat with you.*

Dr Fforde, wishing her good morning later on that day,
noted that she had been crying, but her ordinary face,
rather pink in the nose and puffed around the eyes, was
composed.

'I have had a letter from my aunt, explaining that you
have been to see her and inviting me to stay until I've
another job.'

And when he didn't answer, but stood quietly, watching
her, she said, 'I expect it would be more convenient to you
if I go and stay with her. So may I leave on Saturday? I
expect Miss Priss would like to come as soon as it can be
arranged.' She gave him a brave smile which tore at his
heart. 'If I go early on Saturday morning she could have
the weekend to move in. I'll leave everything ready for
her.'

'That sounds admirable. I will drive you down to your
aunt on Saturday morning.'

She said quickly, 'No, no. There's no need. I haven't
much luggage and I'm sure there is a splendid train service.'

'None the less I will drive you and Sam, Loveday.'

She knew better than to argue when he spoke in that
quiet voice.

'Well, thank you. And if you will write and let me know
if you hear of a job?' She added hastily, 'Oh, I'm sure you
will, because you said so, but I could always go to Exeter.
There is sure to be something there...'

She looked very young standing there, and he was so
much older. He was sure she probably thought of him as

middle-aged. He said gently, 'If you would trust me, Love-day…'

'Oh, I do. You must know that.'

He smiled then, and went to his consulting room.

Loveday and he would be leaving, she told Sam, and she bought a cat basket which he viewed with suspicion. He was suspicious too when she started to spring-clean the flat. The little place must be left pristine, she told herself.

It kept her busy when she wasn't at work, so that she was tired enough to sleep for at least part of the night, but waking in the early hours of the morning there was nothing else to do but go over and over her problems.

The greatest of these, she quickly discovered, was how she was going to live without seeing the doctor each day. She supposed that she hadn't thought much about it before; he was always there, each day, and she had accepted that, not looking ahead. Even when she had supposed her heart to be broken by Charles there had always been the thought that the doctor was there, quiet in the background of her muddled mind.

He had become part of her life without her realising it and now there was nothing to be done about it. Falling in love, she discovered, wasn't anything like the infatuation she had had for Charles. It was the slow awareness of knowing that you wanted to be with someone for the rest of your life…

The days passed too quickly. She packed her small pos-sessions, scoured the flat once more, said goodbye to Todd, and left the waiting room in a state of perfection and the filing cabinet in perfect order.

At the doctor's quiet request she presented herself with her case and Sam in his basket sharp on Saturday morning at nine o'clock. Somehow the leaving was made easier by the fact that he had told her to leave anything she wouldn't need at her aunt's, in the attic next to the flat. It seemed to her a kind of crack in the door, as it were.

With Sam grumbling in his basket on the back seat and Bob beside him, they set off. The doctor had bidden her a cheerful good morning, observing that it should be a pleasant trip.

'I have always liked the late autumn,' he told her, 'even though the days are short. You've brought warm clothing with you? Miss West has a charming house, and the village is just as charming, but it is rather remote—though I believe there's a bus service to Ashburton once a week.' He glanced sideways at her small profile and added cheerfully, 'Probably you won't be there long enough to try it out.'

'You haven't heard of anything that I could do?' she asked, then added quickly, 'I'm sorry. There was no need for me to say that. How can you have had the time? I thought that if there is nothing after a week or ten days I could go into Exeter and look around for a job there.'

'A good idea,' said the doctor, not meaning a word of it. He knew exactly what he was going to do.

They stopped for coffee at a small wayside café on the A303, and Bob, his legs out of plaster now, went for a careful walk. Sam in his basket, somnolent after a big breakfast, hardly stirred.

It was impossible to feel unhappy; the man she had discovered that she loved was here beside her. Perhaps after today she might not see him again, but just for the moment she was happy. They didn't talk much, but when they did it was to discover that they liked the same things—the country, books, animals, winter evenings by the fire, walking in the moonlight. Oh, I do hope Mrs Seward likes the same things, thought Loveday. I want him to be happy.

They stopped for lunch at a hotel a few miles short of

Exeter and then went on their way again—on the Plymouth road now, until they reached Ashburton and turned away from the main road and presently reached the village.

Miss West had the door open before the doctor had stopped the car in front of it. He got out, opened Loveday's door and tucked her hand in his.

'Your niece Loveday, Miss West,' he said.

CHAPTER FIVE

LOVEDAY had grown more and more silent the nearer they had got to Buckland-in-the Moor. It had been a grey overcast day, and once they had left Ashburton behind the moor had stretched before them, magnificent and remote. She had had the nasty feeling that she shouldn't have come; her aunt might not like her, the doctor might not be able to find her another job and, worst of all, she might never see him again.

The lane they'd been driving along had taken a sharp bend and there before them had been the village, tucked beside the river Dart, and as though there had been a prearranged signal a beam of watery sunshine had escaped from the cloud.

'It's beautiful,' Loveday had said, and had suddenly felt much better. She'd turned to look at the doctor.

'I knew you would like it, Loveday,' he had said quietly, but he hadn't looked as he'd driven into the cluster of cottages, past the church, and stopped at Miss West's house.

She'd said in sudden panic, 'You won't go…?'

'No, I shall spend the night at the pub and drive back tomorrow.'

She had let out a small sigh of relief and got out when he'd opened her door, then stood for a moment looking at her aunt's home. There was no front garden, only a grass verge, and at this time of year the grey stone walls looked bleak and unwelcoming, but she had forgotten that when the door had opened and her aunt had stood there with a welcome warm enough to cheer the faintest heart.

Now in the narrow hall, she stopped to study Loveday. 'Your mother had green eyes,' she observed. 'I'm glad that we shall have the chance to get to know each other. You may call me Aunt Leticia.'

She turned to the doctor. 'You had a good journey?' She looked past him. 'The cat and your dog? They are in the car?'

'A very pleasant drive. Bob and Sam are in the car.'

'Good. There is a conservatory leading from the kitchen; Sam may go there for the moment. There is food—everything that he may need. Bob may come into the sitting room.'

She was urging Loveday before her and said over her shoulder, 'Her cases can wait; we will have tea. Take your coats off.'

Loveday did as she was told, and the doctor, amused, did the same, with a nostalgic memory of a fierce, much loved nanny speaking to him in just such a voice.

They had tea, a proper tea, sitting at a round table under the windows while the dogs and cats lay in a companionable heap before the fire. Presently a cautious Sam crept in and joined them, and since none of the animals did more than open an eye he settled down with all the appearance of someone who had come home...

The doctor fetched the cases presently and took his leave, but not before Aunt Leticia had bidden him to Sunday lunch.

'I attend Matins on Sunday mornings,' she told him, 'but I'm sure that you and Loveday will wish to discuss her future. A good walk in the fresh air will do you both good. Fetch her at ten o'clock. You can walk across to Holne and have coffee there. Lunch will be at one o'clock and then she and I will go to Evensong.'

The doctor, recognising an ally, agreed meekly, thanked the old lady for his tea, said a cheerful goodnight to Loveday and took himself and Bob off to the pub, where he was welcomed like an old friend. And later, after a good supper and a quick walk with Bob, he went to bed and slept the sleep of a man untroubled by his future.

Loveday, having repressed a strong desire to run out of the house after him, followed her aunt upstairs to a little room overlooking the back garden and the moor beyond. It was austerely furnished, and had the look of not having had an occupant for a long time, but there were books on the bedside table and a vase of chrysanthemums on the old-fashioned dressing table, and when she was left to unpack her things and opened the wardrobe and stiff drawers there was the delightful scent of lavender.

She went downstairs presently and helped to feed the cats and Tim, surprised to find that Sam seemed quite at home.

'I have always found animals better friends than people,' said Aunt Leticia, 'and they know that. When you go into the garden take care; there is a family of hedgehogs in the compost heap and rabbits in the hedge.'

They spent a pleasant evening together, looking at old photos of family Loveday scarcely remembered, and then, over their supper, Miss West began asking careful questions.

Loveday, enjoying the luxury of having someone to talk to, told her about Miss Cattell and then the doctor. Talking about him made him seem nearer, and her aunt, looking at her niece's ordinary face, saw how it lighted up when she talked of him.

Well, reflected Miss West, Loveday was an ice child. No looks worth mentioning, but with eyes like that looks didn't matter. The doctor was a good deal older, of course, but she didn't think that would matter in the least. He was clearly in love and suspected that Loveday was too, but for some reason she was denying it, even to herself. Ah, well, thought Miss West wisely, all that's needed is a little patience—and absence makes the heart grow fonder…

Loveday, with Sam for company, slept dreamlessly. Her last thoughts had been of the doctor and were the first on waking too. He would go away today, but there was the morning first…

She got up, dressed and went downstairs. She helped get the breakfast and saw to the animals and her aunt, who had liked her on sight, found the liking turning to affection. Loveday was a sensible girl who made no fuss and helped around the house without making a song and dance about it. She'll make Dr Fforde a good wife, reflected Aunt Leticia.

The doctor knocked on the door at ten o'clock, and after a few minutes chatting with Miss West he marched Loveday off at a brisk pace. Bob had come with him but he had already had a walk and now he was sitting contentedly in the sitting room with Tim. As the doctor explained, a long walk would be too tiring for his weak legs.

'Holne is about a mile away,' he told Loveday as they took the narrow road past the church. 'I'm told that we can get coffee there at the pub. Then we can follow the river towards Widecombe. There's a path.'

He began to talk about everything and nothing, with not a word about the future, and because she was so happy with him she forgot for the moment that she had no future and chatted away about the dogs and cats and the hedgehogs in the garden.

'I do like my aunt,' she told him. 'It must be difficult for her to have me living with her, even for a few days; she's lived alone for a long time and she told me that she was happy to be on her own. I expect she knows everyone in the village—she doesn't seem lonely.'

'I'm sure she will enjoy your company. Here's Holne and the pub—shall we stop for coffee?'

The coffee was excellent and there was a great log fire in the bar, but they didn't stay too long. They took the path close to the river and now it was the doctor's turn to tell her about his own life. Oh, yes, he told her when she asked, he had a mother, living in Lincolnshire where his father had had a practice before he died. 'And sisters,' he went on. 'You have met Margaret at the consulting room.'

Loveday came to a halt. 'I thought that she—that you— well, I thought you were going to marry her.'

She went red, although she looked him in the face.

He didn't allow himself to smile. So that was why she had pokered up... Another obstacle out of the way, he reflected. First Charles and now this. The temptation to take her in his arms there and then was great, but there was one more obstacle—the difference in their ages. He must give her time to think about that...

He said lightly, 'I've always been too busy to get married.' They were walking on now. 'And you, Loveday, have you no wish to marry?'

'Yes, but only to the right man.' She didn't want to talk about that. 'Do you suppose we should be turning back?'

He accepted her change in the conversation without comment.

They walked back the way they had come and the chilly bright morning began to cloud over. When they were within sight of the cottage, Loveday said, 'You will let me know…? I'm sorry to keep reminding you, but I'd like to be certain.'

'I promise you that I will let you know, and now that we are no longer working together could you not call me Andrew?'

She smiled suddenly. 'I've always called you Andrew inside my head,' she told him.

Lunch was a cheerful meal. Aunt Leticia might live alone, but she was aware of all that went on in the world so far removed from her home. There was plenty to talk about—until she said reluctantly, 'You will want to be on your way, and I mustn't keep you. Loveday, get your coat and walk up to the pub and see Dr Fforde safely away.'

The walk was short—far too short. Only a matter of a couple of minutes. Loveday stood by the car while the doctor invited Bob onto the back seat, closed the car door and turned to her.

He took her hands in his and stood looking down at her. The scarf she had tied over her mousy locks had done nothing to enhance her appearance. She looked about sixteen years old, and the last obstacle, the difference in their ages, was suddenly very real. He would marry her, but not until she had had the chance to lead her own life to meet people—young men—who would make her laugh as Charles had done.

All the things he wanted to say were unsaid. He wished her goodbye and got into the car and drove away.

She watched it through tear-filled eyes until it disappeared round the curve in the lane. Just for a moment she had thought that he was going to say something—that he would see her again, that they would keep in touch, remain friends…

She wiped her eyes and went back to Aunt Leticia. She helped with the washing up and then took the elderly Tim for his ambling walk, and later went to Evensong with her aunt. No one, looking at her quiet face, would have guessed how unhappy she was.

The days which followed were quiet, centred round the simple life Aunt Leticia lived, but there was always something to do. She often walked to Holne, a mile away, where there was a Post Office, and to the nearby farm for eggs, and halfway through each week she was sent to Ashburton on the weekly bus, armed with a shopping list—groceries and meat, wool for her aunt's knitting, and food for the cats and Tim. There was the weekly excitement of the travelling library, and the daily collecting of the newspapers from the pub.

The landlord liked a good gossip in his slow friendly voice; he was too kind a man to ask questions, but life in the village was quiet and her arrival had made a nice little break now that there were no visitors passing through. He had taken to the doctor, too, and had several times confided in his wife that there was more to his visits than met the eye...

It was late on a Saturday evening by the time the doctor arrived at the pub. It was too late to call on Miss West, so it was early on Sunday morning when Loveday got up to let Tim and the cats out and saw him coming down the lane.

She ran to the door and flung it wide as he reached it, and went into his arms with the unselfconsciousness of a child.

He closed the door gently behind them and then wrapped his arms around her again.

'I had to come. I had to know. You see, my darling Loveday, I'm in love with you...'

'Then why didn't you say so?' she asked fiercely.

'I'm so much older than you, and you have never had the chance to meet men of your own age. Only Charles.'

She dismissed Charles with a sniff. 'Is that your only reason?' She hesitated. 'I'm dull and plain and not at all clever. I'd be a very unexciting wife for someone like you.'

'I find you very exciting,' he told her, and kissed her, and presently said, 'You shall have all the time in the world to decide if you will marry me. I'll go back to London this evening and not come again until you can give me an answer.'

She looked at him then, and said in a shaky little voice, 'I'll stay here as long as you want me to, but I'll give you my answer now. I love you too, and I'll marry you—today if we could.'

He looked down at her earnest, loving face and smiled. Fourteen years were nothing; they simply didn't matter. He kissed her again, very thoroughly—a delightful experience which, naturally enough, was repeated.

Aunt Leticia, coming downstairs to put the kettle on made no effort to disturb them. Putting tea leaves into the teapot, she reflected that she would give them the silver pot which had belonged to her great-great-grandmother for a wedding present. She took her tea and sat by the Aga, waiting patiently. Let them have their lovely moment.

A SPECIAL KIND
OF WOMAN

Caroline Anderson

Dear Reader,

This story was written from the heart. At the end of September we took our elder daughter to college in London for the first time, and it was *awful!* I didn't cry then. I don't know why not, except perhaps that I had missed the point. I discovered it with a vengeance five days later, and howled for hours. I still miss her, weeks later, but writing the story helped to work it out of my system.

I am hugely fortunate. I have my husband—her father—with me to share the ups and downs of parenting. Sadly many people don't.

Cait didn't, and nor did Owen—so I gave them each other. Wasn't that kind of me? I am such a nice person! I hope you enjoy their story. I'm sure it will strike a chord in the heart of all the "empty nesters" out there who, like us, have struggled to come to terms with this phase of life. Still, one down, one to go, and then people tell me there are huge benefits—tidy house, romantic weekends away, candlelit dinners....

I'll keep you posted!

Best wishes,

Caroline Anderson

CHAPTER ONE

'THAT'S it, there.'

Cait looked up at the grim and forbidding exterior of the halls of residence and her heart sank. Oh, lord. Her baby was going to be living here in this dismal grey pile, hemmed in by endless buildings and concrete and dirt and vice—

'Look, Mum, there's a parking place, by that Mercedes.'

So there was. What an unfortunate contrast. She zipped her modest old banger across the road into the space just ahead of another car, triggering a blast on the horn and wild gestures the meaning of which she could only guess at.

She resisted the urge to gesture back, and reversed neatly into place behind the Mercedes. 'OK. I wonder if we've got enough money to feed the meter and keep it quiet for an hour or so?'

'It won't take that long,' Milly said naïvely. 'I've only got a few things.'

Cait glanced in the rear-view mirror at the teetering pile of essentials Milly had simply *had* to bring with her, and sighed. A few things? In her dreams.

She fed the meter—copiously—and then they had to run the gauntlet of the security system to gain access to the entrance hall. Milly went up to the porter behind his desk in the porter's lodge and smiled a little uncertainly. 'Hi. I'm Emily Cooper. I've got a room here this year?'

'Sure. Cooper—here it is. Here's your swipe card, your

room key, information about the phone system, rules of the hall...'

He handed over a sheaf of papers, rattled off some instructions and dropped the key in Milly's outstretched hand. 'Give me a shout if you need any help.'

'Right, let's go and have a look,' Cait said. 'We'll bring in your things in a minute.' She summoned up an encouraging smile, and Milly smiled back, her face a little tight and pale.

To be fair, it was probably pale because of all the wild partying and farewells that had been going on for the past few days, but Cait knew she was also apprehensive.

It was a huge step in her life, and one Cait had no personal experience of to fall back on in her encouragement. She couldn't give her the 'don't do this and you'll enjoy that and try the other' sort of talk she might have been able to under other circumstances, because she'd never made it to university, despite her ambition to read Law. Instead she'd been struggling to raise Emily and keep a roof over their heads.

Not that she'd ever been as clever as her brilliant and multi-talented daughter. Still, she'd done her best for her, kept her nose to the grindstone and been there for her for the last eighteen years.

And now it was time to let go.

Oh, help.

'It looks quite decent,' Milly said slowly, as if she was trying to convince herself. 'At least the paint's new.'

On old and crumbling walls, Cait thought with a return of her maternal panic. Oh, yipes. She dredged up a smile. 'Here's your room! Look, it's handy for the kitchen. That'll be nice.'

'Not when everyone's making tea in the middle of the

night,' Milly said pragmatically and shoved her key in the lock.

The door swung open to reveal a fairly small and barren room. Although like the corridor outside it had been recently decorated, still it seemed bare and forbidding, and Cait's heart sank. There was a bed, a chair, a battered old desk with some wonky shelves over it, a wardrobe in the corner and that was it. Home from home it was not, even though their home was far from luxurious. Poor baby.

'Well, at least it's clean, and the carpet's new, by the look of it,' she said with false cheer. 'What's the bed like?'

Milly bounced experimentally. 'OK. Bit soft.' She stood up and looked out of the window into an inner courtyard, and her face fell. What a dismal view, Cait thought. The bins. Oh, lord.

'At least you won't have the traffic noise from the street,' she said bracingly, and Milly made a small noise that might have been agreement. 'Come on, let's get your things and you can unpack and put everything out on the shelves. It'll look a lot better then.'

Milly made the same noncommittal noise, and with an inward sigh Cait followed her back out to the car. They brought in the cases first, bumping and banging on their legs and the walls of the corridor, and as they struggled up the stairs to the second floor, they had to pause to let two people pass.

The man went first, tall and rugged, flashing her a brief, impersonal smile of thanks that for some reason made her heart beat faster, then a young man Cait thought was probably his son paused beside Emily.

'Hey—Milly, isn't it?' he said, and Milly flipped her hair out of her eyes.

'Hi, Josh!' she exclaimed, and smiled up at him with every appearance of delight. 'What are you doing here?'

'Same as you, I guess.' He lounged against the stairwell wall and grinned. 'So, did you make it to medicine?'

'Yes—did you?'

'Yeah—hey, that's really cool!' His grin widened, and Milly's smile lit up her face.

She's really beautiful, Cait thought with a lump in her throat. Oh, heck. Will she be all right?

'Josh?'

The voice echoed back up the corridor, and he pulled a face. 'Coming!' he called, and flashed her another grin. 'I'll see you around, Milly.' He bounded down the stairs two at a time and disappeared round the corner.

Cait watched him go, tall and gangly but with a cheerful friendliness about him that lightened her spirits. 'So who was that?' she asked Milly casually.

'Oh, his name's Josh something—can't remember. He was at one of the other schools in town—I've seen him around. He went out with Jo for a bit. I met him on a conference in Cambridge as well, but I haven't seen him for ages.'

'Well, it's someone you know, anyway,' Cait said, relieved as much for herself as for her daughter. 'It's always nice to see a familiar face, and he seemed pleased to see you. Come on, let's get these bags in.'

The bags were the easy bit. The boxes were much more of a challenge, and Cait was wondering how on earth she was going to get up the stairs with the last one, a hugely awkward lump that seemed determined to defeat her, when she felt the weight taken out of her hands.

'Here, let me,' a soft, deep voice murmured.

'Thanks.' She stepped back and smiled, then their eyes

net and her heart hiccuped behind her ribs. 'Oh—you're
osh's father,' she said inanely.

'That's right. Owen Douglas.'

'I'm Milly's mother—Cait Cooper.'

'Her *mother*? Good heavens. I thought you were her
sister or aunt or something.'

Flattery? If it weren't for the wedding ring on his hand
and the fact that *he* was helping *her*, not the other way
round, she would have thought he wanted something. Under the circumstances she gave him the benefit of the doubt
and blamed it on the poor lighting.

'Hardly,' she said, studying him and thinking what a
terrible shame it was that he was married. Not that he'd
be interested in her. No man worth having ever was. Oh,
well.

He flashed her a rueful smile over the top of the box
that nearly melted the soles of her shoes. 'I'd shake your
hand but I seem to be holding something just a tad heavy
at the moment.'

'Oh, my goodness, I'm sorry!' She leapt to attention.
'Can you manage it?'

'I think I'll just about cope,' he said drily. 'You'll have
to show me the way, though.'

'Of course—she's on the second floor,' she told him
over her shoulder, heading up the stairs at a fast clip. 'Josh
must be on the floor above.'

'He is. I think he's giving Milly a tour at the moment.
We've finished, at last. I can't believe he thinks he needs
this much.'

Cait laughed. 'We're not the only ones, then? I'm sure
most of what you're struggling with is non-essential.'

'Nothing's essential,' he said drily. 'Not by the time
you've lugged it up three flights of stairs.'

He lowered the box to the last square inch of space on Milly's floor, and straightened with a smile, holding out his hand. He must be fit, she thought. He isn't even breathing hard.

'It's good to meet you, Cait,' he said, and belatedly she reached out her hand and felt it totally engulfed in a warm, hard grip that robbed her of her senses. She mumbled something about small worlds, and he laughed.

'Not really. There aren't that many medical schools— you're almost bound to meet someone you know.'

'Well, I'm very glad we met you! Quite apart from you lugging that huge box upstairs for me, it's comforting to know she's not totally alone in this big, bad city.'

He shot her an understanding smile. His eyes crinkled and seemed to glow with warmth from their amber depths, and she felt herself melting again. She could still feel the imprint of his hand on hers, and something deep in her heart that had been in hibernation for ever seemed to flicker into life.

How long they stood there staring at each other she didn't know, but Milly and Josh erupted into the room and broke the spell, and a girl opposite came out and introduced herself, and suddenly Cait felt redundant.

'Time to make a move,' Owen murmured, and she nodded distractedly.

'Come on, Josh, come and see me off,' he said, and his son's face seemed to falter.

'Oh. Right. See you, Milly.'

Milly nodded, and the girl from the next room looked from her to Cait and said she'd see Milly later, and went out, leaving them alone.

'Want me to help you unpack?' Cait asked, not knowing

whether to prolong the agony or get the heck out of it before she made a fool of herself.

'I can manage,' Milly said. 'It'll give me something to do until teatime.'

'Now, the phone in here should be working for me to ring in, they said, so I'll call you when I'm home, and you've got your mobile if you need me—'

'It's OK, Mum. I'll be fine.' She hugged Cait, and Cait wrapped her arms around her and thought how slight Milly felt, how small and slender and fragile and much too little to be here, doing this all on her own.

'Right, I'll be off before I get a parking ticket,' she said brightly, and kissed Milly on the cheek. 'Remember, I'm there if you need me. Love you.'

She hugged her daughter again, a brief, hard hug, and then turned and made her way sightlessly through the corridors and out into the street. The Mercedes was gone, so she backed into the space, pulled out into the street and made her way out into the hum of the London traffic.

I won't cry, she told herself firmly, and then again out loud, 'I won't cry! She's doing what she wants to do. She's happy! She's made it. There's nothing to cry about.'

But there was, of course, because her baby had grown up and flown the nest, and now Cait would be all alone.

'You'll be able to do what you've always wanted to do. You've enrolled for that course in Law, and you can read books and go to films and museums and art galleries, and do all the things you've never had time for.'

Intellectual things. Not family things. She'd be clever and better educated, but she'd be *lonely*.

She sniffed hard and scrubbed her cheeks on the back of her hand, then had to dig about in her pocket for a tissue. She wandered into the next lane and got a blast on a horn for her pains, and after that she turned on the radio and sang to it, very loudly and utterly off key, all the way out of London onto the A12.

Then finally her bravado fizzled out, and she turned off at a roadside restaurant, folded her arms on the steering wheel and laid her head down and howled.

'Idiot,' she told herself disparagingly a few minutes later. 'You must look a total fright.'

She lifted her head, blew her nose vigorously and glared at herself in the rear-view mirror. Red-rimmed, bloodshot eyes glared back at her, and she sighed unsteadily. 'Coffee,' she said, and opened the car door, to find Owen Douglas standing there, immaculately clad legs crossed at the ankle, propping up a familiar Mercedes estate.

'You OK?' he said softly, and she closed her eyes in despair. Of all the times to bump into someone you didn't know well enough to howl on.

'I'll live,' she muttered, and forced herself to meet his eyes. They were gentle with understanding, and suddenly she was glad he was there because, know him or not, he was at least in the same boat.

'You look like I feel,' he said with a rueful smile. 'How about a coffee?'

She nodded. 'I was just going in. Have you only just arrived?'

He shook his head. 'No, I was leaving. I'm in no hurry, though, and I'm sure I could force down another cup. You know what they say about misery loving company.'

Her laugh was a little strangled, and it ended on something suspiciously like a sob, but at least it was a laugh, and maybe she'd cried enough.

'Coffee sounds good,' she said, and for the first time in hours, she managed a genuine smile. 'Thanks.'

'My pleasure,' he murmured, and his voice sent little fingers of anticipation shivering up and down her spine.

Don't be a fool, he's married, she told herself fiercely, but his eyes were smiling and her heart was clearly not listening at all...

CHAPTER TWO

SHE looks gutted, Owen thought as they headed towards the restaurant. Empty and hollow and a little lost, just how he felt. He held the door for Cait and caught a drift of scent—not really perfume, just a subtle trace of something tantalising mingled with the warmth of her skin.

The waiter came up to him, looking puzzled. 'Did you leave something behind, sir?' he asked, and Owen shook his head.

'No. I've just bumped into a friend and decided to come back,' he said, and then wondered if it were rather over-stating the case to call her a friend. Probably. A slight acquaintance was nearer the mark.

Very slight.

And yet he felt he knew her, because they were sharing the same very real and basic emotions at the moment and that gave them an instant connection.

He ushered her to a seat, his hand resting lightly on the smooth, supple curve of her spine, and as they sat down opposite each other she flashed him a small but potent smile that hit him right in the solar plexus.

'Thank you for rescuing me,' she said softly. 'I hate coming into places like this alone, but I couldn't go on any longer without...'

She trailed off, so he finished the sentence for her. 'Letting go?' he suggested. His grin felt crooked. 'Been there, done that.'

Cait searched his face with her luminous grey eyes, and he wondered if the few renegade tears that had escaped his rigid control had left their mark. So what if they had? he decided. He loved his son. After all they'd been through together, Josh was worthy of his tears.

'Are you OK?' she asked gently, and he gave a soft grunt of laughter.

'I'll do,' he said with a sigh, and she smiled back, tucking her long dark hair behind her ears and fiddling with her watchstrap.

'Hell, isn't it?' she said. 'I've spent years working towards this with her, and now it's come I feel—oh, I don't know what I feel.'

'Oh, I do,' he said with heartfelt sympathy. 'I know exactly how you feel.'

Her smile was a bit wonky. 'Oh, well. At least you didn't make an ass of yourself in the car park,' she told him drily, and he chuckled.

'I wouldn't bet on it.'

The waiter came up to them, pad in hand, and asked if they were ready to order.

'Coffee?' Owen suggested, and she nodded.

'Please.'

'Anything else? We could always eat if you're hungry.'

He met her eyes, those lovely soft grey eyes with the dark line defining the iris. Her skin was clear, her lips soft and mobile, and he had an insane urge to kiss them. Just now they were moving, saying something, and he had to pull himself together almost physically. 'Sorry, I didn't catch that,' he said, and she gave him an odd look.

Dear me, you're losing it, Owen, old chum, he told himself, and felt heat crawl up his neck.

'I said, I don't want to hold you up,' Cait repeated. 'Won't your wife be waiting for you?'

Jill. His embarrassment faded, replaced by the ache of an old, familiar sadness.

He shook his head. 'No. No, she won't be waiting,' he said softly. 'What about you? Will there be someone waiting for you?'

She shook her head. Something flickered briefly in her eyes that found an echo in his lonely soul. It was replaced by her slightly off-kilter smile. 'No. No one's waiting for me, except the cat, and she can cope.'

'So—how about it?'

'I tell you what, I'll bring your coffee while you decide,' the waiter said, giving up on them and handing them a menu each. Owen felt a twinge of guilt. He'd forgotten the man's existence.

'Thanks,' he murmured, and raised a brow at Cait. 'Well?'

She looked down at the menu, then up at him again. 'Um—if you've got time, I wouldn't mind something light.'

'Have whatever. I'm going for a truly wicked fry-up.'

Her eyes widened, and then she laughed, a low, musical sound that played hell with his composure. 'Comfort food?' she said wryly, and he chuckled.

'Something like that. Plus I don't have Josh nagging me. He's a health-food freak. How he'll survive in halls I can't imagine.'

'Milly will be in clover. My cooking's hit and miss at the best of times, and most of the time I'm too busy to worry. I can't remember when I last cooked anything like a roast—well, apart from last night, but it was sort of the Last Supper and the Prodigal Son all rolled into one, if you get my drift.'

He did. He'd done just the same thing, only they'd gone out to a restaurant and then on to a pub and caught a taxi home, both a little the worse for wear and a bit subdued this morning.

The waiter brought their coffee, and Owen poured them both a cup and sat back, stirring his cream in absently and thinking about Josh and how odd it was going to be at home without him.

'So, what do you do that keeps you so busy?' he asked with deliberate cheer, changing the subject, and she laughed and rolled her eyes.

'I've got a shop, for my sins—I hire and make ball gowns, and occasionally wedding dresses. It's a bit seasonal, but there's usually a steady flow of work. The balls are winter and the weddings are summer, in the main, so it pans out quite well. What about you?'

'I'm a doctor—a surgeon,' he told her. 'I cut up people instead of fabric. It's easier than your job. People heal.'

It made Cait laugh. 'True, but I can buy new fabric if I make a mess, and I can always make a mock-up,' she pointed out, and he smiled.

'I'll have to concede that one. I can't see me waking a patient up and saying, "OK, that was just a dummy run, now we'll do the real thing."'

Her smile was gorgeous. Too wide, really, but her teeth were even and sparkling, and her nose wrinkled up when she laughed. She really used the whole of her face. Every muscle of it was involved in her spontaneous expressions.

She'd be a lousy poker player, Owen thought slowly, but she'd be incredible to make love to. Every touch, every stroke would find an echo in that wonderfully mobile face and those incredible eyes.

He shifted slightly in his seat, aware of the stirrings of a need he hadn't felt in years. She worried her bottom lip with her teeth, and his breath jammed in his lungs. He dragged his eyes from her face and down to the menu, scanning it blindly for a moment until his eyes focused.

Then he chose the most wicked thing he could find and stuck the menu back in the holder.

'I'm ready when you are,' he told her, his voice sounding strangled, and the double meaning hit him like a tram. Oh, hell. He hoped she wasn't looking at him, because for a brief, terrifying second he was sure his thoughts were clearly written on his face—and they were seriously, seriously X-rated!

Cait was starving.

Owen had chosen what he was having and had put his menu down, but she was torn between the toast and pâté she'd spotted at first and the wonderful illustration of golden crispy chicken and chips with a side salad. It was horribly expensive by comparison, but what the heck. She could afford to splash out every once in a while, and it was a rather unique occasion, if not exactly special in the accepted sense!

'I can't decide,' she murmured, but her eyes strayed back to the chicken and chips. 'I was going to have the pâté, but this looks so tempting…'

'Go for it,' he advised, taking the menu out of her hand. 'Stop worrying. Instinct is a wonderful thing.'

'So it is. OK, I'll go for it.'

She looked up into his face, but it was expressionless, apart from a polite smile that told her nothing. He hailed the waiter, ordered their meal and topped up her coffee.

She stirred the cream into it, chasing a bubble round the top, and then looked up at him again, surprising an unguarded look that made her breath catch in her throat.

No. She was imagining it. Of course he hadn't looked at her like that.

'So, where do you live?' she asked to fill the silence, and then wondered if that was too intrusive a question to ask on such brief acquaintance. Apparently not, because Owen volunteered the information without a flicker.

'Just south of Audley—about ten miles out, a little bit west of Wenham Market.'

'That's near me,' she said, and wondered if she sounded hopelessly over-eager. That would be embarrassing. Just because he'd said there was no one waiting that didn't mean there was no one in his life. Maybe she was away, perhaps on business. Oh, blast.

'Near you?' he said. 'The shop or your house?'

'Both. That's where the shop is, in the square, between the antique shop and the butcher, and we live in the flat above it.'

'It's a nice little town—or is it a village?'

Cait laughed softly. 'I don't know. I'm not sure they can decide. We've got a village hall, but it's quite big for a village and it's got lots of shops. I'd say it was more of a town, in a way.'

'It's got lots of character. I envy you in a way. It's a bit isolated where we are. It's all part of its essential charm, but it's also one of the greatest drawbacks.'

'Is it an old house?' she asked, slightly appalled at her curiosity, but he didn't seem to mind.

'Yes and no,' he said confusingly, and then elaborated with a smile. 'It's a converted barn—so the barn itself is old, but it's only been a house for a short while. Six years or so, I think. I bought it three years ago, after my wife died.'

Cait felt shock run over her like iced water. Not away on business, then, she thought numbly, and shook her head in denial. 'Oh, Owen, I'm so sorry,' she murmured.

'Why should you be sorry?' he said softly. 'It's just one of those things. It was quick, at least. She didn't suffer.

She had a burst blood vessel in the brain—she must have died almost instantly.'

'Oh, Owen,' she said again. 'How awful for you. Was she at home?'

'No. She was in the car. She'd pulled over but the engine was still running. A witness said she pulled up, slumped over and that was it. They discovered the haemorrhage at post-mortem.'

How hideous for them. How horribly sudden and violent and unexpected. She felt tears prickle at the back of her eyes and blinked them away. 'It must have been dreadful,' she said, choked. 'How did Josh take it?'

Owen laughed, a short, humourless huff of sound. 'Not well. He was fourteen at the time. He was furious with her.'

'And the others—are there any others?'

He shook his head. 'No. No others. Just me and Josh.'

'Chicken and chips?'

They both looked up, slightly startled, to see the waiter hovering over them with two plates.

'Um—yes, thank you,' Cait said, moving her cup out of the way and letting his revelation sink in. The waiter left them, and without thinking she reached out her hand and covered his. 'Owen—thanks for telling me about it.'

His grin was crooked and a little off-key. 'That's OK. I don't usually talk about it. I'm sorry to unravel on you like that. I shouldn't have brought it up.'

'Yes, you should. She was a part of your life for years. You can't just not talk about her as if she didn't exist.'

He met her steady gaze, gratitude at her understanding showing in his amber eyes, and then he smiled a little sadly. 'Thank you for that. You're right, but most people don't see it that way. It makes them uncomfortable.'

'That's silly.'

'Maybe. Eat your chicken and chips.'

She looked at his plate, heaped with what looked for all the world like a truly wicked Sunday breakfast, and had a sudden urge to dunk her chip in his egg yolk.

'Go on, then, if you must.'

'What?' She looked up, startled, to find him laughing softly at her.

'Dunk your chips in my egg.'

The smile wouldn't be held in. 'That's so rude of me. How did you know?'

'Something to do with the longing look you gave it?'

Oh, lord. She'd better not direct any longing looks at *him*, then. He was altogether too good at picking them up!

She reached over, the chip in her fingers, and pierced the golden yolk. 'Oh, yum,' she mumbled round the mouthful, and he laughed again.

'One more, and that's your lot,' he said firmly, and she indulged herself one last time before turning her attention to the fragrant, steaming plateful of chicken in front of her.

Within a few minutes she'd demolished it, and sat back with a huge sigh of contentment. 'Oh, wow,' she said with a grin. 'Excellent.'

He speared the last mushroom and chewed it thoughtfully, then smiled back. 'How about a pud?'

'That's too wicked!' She laughed. 'Anyway, I'll burst.'

'How horribly messy. We'd better avoid that at all costs. Another coffee?'

She shook her head, reality coming back to her. She had work to do before she opened the shop in the morning, and it was already after seven. Besides, the cat would be hungry and would take the hump and go off in a sulk if she didn't get back soon.

'I ought to go,' she told him, and he nodded.

'OK.' He looked up and caught the waiter's eye, and a bill appeared a moment later.

'Could you please split it?' she asked him, but Owen shook his head.

'No. Leave it. Here.' He counted out a pile of notes, told the man to keep the change and ushered her out.

'You shouldn't have done that,' she protested, but he just smiled.

'Yes, I should. I talked you into it—and, anyway, it was a pleasure having your company.' He walked her to her car, and as she reached it he looked down into her eyes and searched them in silence for a moment.

'Thank you for rescuing me from the doldrums,' she said, a touch breathlessly, and he smiled, just a slight shift of his lips in the harsh glare of the outside lights. His eyes were in shadow, but they seemed to burn with an inner fire that she didn't dare interpret.

'My pleasure,' he murmured, and before she could move or speak or even blink, he bent his head and brushed her lips with his. 'Goodnight, Cait. Take care.'

He slipped a card into her hand. 'Here. This is my number. Ring me if you need anything.'

Then he was gone, his long legs striding round his car. He slid behind the wheel and waited for her to get into her car, then once she was settled and pulled forward a fraction, he raised a hand in farewell and followed her out of the car park.

His lights trailed her all the way home, then as she pulled up they flashed a couple of times and he drove away.

How chivalrous, she thought with a tiny smile, and then looked up at the dark window in her flat over the shop. Oh, lord. No Milly to nag and bully and hug. None of her various friends to trip over, no festering coffee-mugs on

Milly's bedroom window-sill, no frenzied searching for a bag, a phone, a piece of paper.

Just silence.

Cait braced herself, and got out of the car. It was time to start the rest of her life.

She slid her hand into her pocket to pull out her house keys, and the sharp corner of Owen's card scratched the palm of her hand. She pulled it out and looked at it in the dim light of the streetlamps, and a smile curved her lips.

Maybe—just maybe—her new life had already started.

CHAPTER THREE

CAIT would have gone crazy in the next few days without
the cat to keep her company. They were both a little lost
without Milly, and to comfort herself poor old Bagpuss
took up residence in Cait's immediate vicinity.

Wherever she was, the cat was too. She slept with her,
she followed her round all day, and she cried piteously if
Cait shut her out.

It was getting on her nerves, but since she could understand it, it was hard to get cross with her.

Well, most of the time. On the second Sunday Milly
was gone, she put down a wedding dress for ten seconds
and came back to find the cat making a nest inside the
piles of tulle.

'Out!' she ordered firmly, not daring to pick the cat up
for fear of plucking the fine netting, and Bagpuss stalked
off with her tail in the air. It didn't last long, though.
Within moments she was back again, scratching at the door
until Cait relented and let her back in.

She jumped up and settled down on the sewing table
next to the pins and bobbins, tucking her paws under her
and purring gloatingly because she'd got her own way
again. Every now and again she reached out an idle paw
and batted at the threads trailing from the needles in the
pin cushion, making Cait nervous. She moved the pin
cushion out of reach.

'I don't need a vet bill,' she said, but the cat just washed
herself and settled down for a snooze. 'Tired?' Cait asked
unfeelingly. 'That's because you were miaowing all night

and keeping me awake. I told you, she's gone. She won't be back for ages. Maybe even Christmas.'

Christmas? Good grief. It seemed such a long time away, but it wasn't really. She was just finishing off this last of a run of wedding dresses, and then she'd have to overhaul her winter ball gowns, all the reds and blacks and deep greens that were so popular for the Christmas balls.

Some would need revamping, others would go in the pre-season sale, and she would have to do a lot of restocking, so she wouldn't have time to miss Milly.

Not really. Only every time she got out two plates for supper, or cooked two jacket potatoes instead of one, or weighed out the wrong amount of spaghetti. Only whenever she went into the bathroom and it was tidy, with no soggy towels dropped on the floor or nightdress abandoned over the edge of the bath or the scales missing.

Only whenever she heard something funny and wanted to share it with her daughter, and then remembered she wasn't there.

She was getting on fine, by all accounts—or at least she seemed to be. She'd rung a couple of times, between one party and another, and she seemed to be having a great time.

Unlike Cait, who was submerged under a pile of tulle that had to be ready by tomorrow.

And then, of course, there was the evening class she'd enrolled herself on.

She sighed. Maybe she was trying to take too much on, but she couldn't afford to get someone else to run the shop and she didn't dare farm out the sewing. She'd tried that before, with disastrous consequences.

So she'd struggle, and she'd probably have to stay up half the night every now and again, but she'd get there.

She had an essay to finish for tomorrow night, come to

that, but her bride was coming for a fitting at nine in the morning, and she had to get the dress to the right stage by then. Still, it was straightforward enough, a variation on a pattern she'd made several times before.

She stayed up until eleven working on it, then started on the essay. Not a good move. Her brain felt like treacle, and the words seemed doubly impenetrable through the fog of exhaustion.

She fell asleep with her head in the book at one, went to bed and tried to carry on, and finally at three she admitted defeat, turned out the light and disappeared into blissful oblivion until eight thirty-eight.

Twenty-two minutes till her fitting.

Great!

She shot out of bed, had the fastest shower in the history of mankind and gave the cat a double portion of food by accident as she rushed out of the flat and downstairs to the shop, the dress carefully held aloft so she didn't trip over it and shred the bottom.

Her bride was late. Almost half an hour late—time for a cup of tea and some toast while she finished off her essay, had she but known, but she didn't, so she spent the whole time waiting for the young woman to arrive.

Still, she got the shop tidied after Saturday's hectic rummaging and started her winter stock check, so the time wasn't exactly wasted, although it was a bit irritating because it was Monday and the shop was shut on Mondays except for fittings and for regular clients who couldn't come on any other day. She could have been having a lie-in, she thought resentfully, or finishing the darned essay.

Her bride arrived, and the dress, by a miracle, was wonderful on her, elegant and flattering to a figure that was less than perfect, and she was ecstatic. Good, Cait thought,

I'll get paid, and then just as she was seeing her off and locking the shop again, a car pulled up outside.

She just caught a glimpse of it out of the corner of her eye, and her heart sank. Not another customer. Not today, when she had the essay to do!

She turned back to the door and her heart zoomed back up out of her boots and started hammering away at the base of her throat.

Owen—here, of all places, out of the blue and unheralded, when she'd just dragged a comb through her wet hair and pulled on the first clean clothes on hand. Why was he always destined to see her at her worst?

She glanced down at her jeans and sweater and shrugged. Perhaps not her very worst. At least the sweater didn't have holes in it and the jeans were the ones that fitted her bottom nicely. Pity about the make-up, but two out of three wasn't bad and it *was* lovely to see him again.

Very lovely. Wonderful, in fact, she realised, as her heart skittered about and did strange things to her insides.

Trying not to grin too inanely, she opened the door again and leant against the doorframe, her arms folded across her chest, one leg resting slightly bent against the other. 'Hi, there,' she said, feeling the smile widen despite her best efforts. 'Don't tell me, you want a ball gown.'

He grinned back. 'Shucks, you guessed. Still, it can be our little secret. I thought something off the shoulder…?'

She felt one eyebrow climb, and her lips twitched. 'Come in, I'll see what I can do for you.'

'Too kind.'

He walked past her into the shop, passing within millimetres of her, and all her senses screamed to full alert. Suddenly the shop seemed absurdly small and crowded.

Cait turned the lock on the door and eyed him blatantly, disguising her sudden confusion with a jokey appraisal of his body. 'Mmm. Those shoulders could be a problem,' she teased, and he smiled.

'Ah, well. Never mind the gown, I'll settle for a coffee.'

A coffee. She had tea, she had hot chocolate. Coffee she was out of—and the kitchen looked as if a bomb had gone off in it. 'Um—' she flannelled, but he cut her off.

'I've got the day off. I just called on spec because I thought you'd be in, but—as you're shut—maybe we could go out—if you'd like to, that is, or you've got time?'

'Out?' she said blankly, and could have kicked herself for sounding so vacant.

'Out—you know, maybe to the seaside or a craft centre or something? I don't know. Whatever you fancy.'

He sounded a little lost, and she tipped her head on one side and studied him thoughtfully. 'You miss him, don't you?'

Owen's mouth kicked up at the side and he gave a short huff of laughter. 'Rumbled,' he said wryly, and searched her face. 'How about you?'

Cait shrugged. 'It seems very odd. She's rung me a couple of times, when she's been able to fit it in—they seem to do nothing but go from one party to another. I can't get her on her room phone at all.'

'Ditto. Josh says the medics really know how to party. I don't think he's been to bed for more than a hour at a time for the last week and a half.' He shoved his hands into his pockets and rocked back on his heels. 'So—fancy playing hookey?'

Her mouth tipped in a slow smile. 'Do I ever,' she said with feeling. 'I have an essay to finish for tonight for my Law evening class, I have to put that wedding dress together now she's had a fitting, and the place is a tip. Oh, yes, I fancy playing hookey—in capitals!'

He laughed. 'Let's go, then.'

'I need to change,' she said, eyeing his suit, but he shook his head.

'No. You're fine. I wish I was wearing something less formal. I hate suits.'

'So why did you put it on?' she asked, puzzled.

'Because my day off was unscheduled. They had to close my theatre because of staff shortages, so my list was cancelled at the last minute. I suppose we could go via my house and I could change. How long can you spare?'

Cait thought of everything she had to do, and then thought of the rest of her life spent doing just that, and smiled defiantly. 'As long as you like.'

He nodded, a smile hovering in his eyes. 'OK. We'll go via mine and I'll change. You can meet the dogs then— are you all right with dogs?'

'I love dogs,' she told him. 'I just can't have one in the flat. The garden's tiny and it's not really fair when I'm at work all day, even if it is just downstairs.'

Owen pulled a thoughtful face and nodded again, slowly. 'I agree. I didn't know what to do about mine when Jill died, but I think they'd probably rather stay with me and put up with my long hours at work than be rehomed, and anyway, I'd miss them. Still, I have a home help who comes in every day for a couple of hours, so it's not too bad.'

Every day, Cait thought enviously. She'd give her eye teeth for someone to come and run a vacuum over the flat once a month, never mind every day. She kept the shop immaculate, but the flat always seemed to run away with her. Ah, well.

'What do I need?' she asked, and he shrugged.

'Coat? Shoes for walking if you fancy walking, or not if you don't. Nothing much.'

She nodded. 'Give me five seconds and I'll be back,'

she said, and then threw over her shoulder as she headed for the door marked PRIVATE, 'You could pick out your ball gown while you're waiting!'

She ran up to the flat, apologised to Bagpuss for deserting her and dithered for a moment over her make-up. No, too obvious, she decided, and grabbed a coat and her trainers and bag and ran back down.

'I thought this one,' he said, holding up a few strips of gold held together with imagination. It was an outrageous gown and just the thought of Owen in it made her lips twitch.

She shook her head. 'No. You need a bigger bust to carry it off,' she told him, deadpan.

He hung it up again, pulling a regretful face, and she laughed.

'Ah, poor baby,' she teased, and his mouth quirked.

'You're a hard woman—I'm sure my bust is big enough for that dress.'

'You'd have to wax your chest, though,' she pointed out wickedly, and he winced.

'Perhaps not, then. I'll stick to the DJ.'

'Might be safer.'

Cait locked the shop behind them, and he settled her into the luxury of the passenger seat before going round and sliding behind the wheel. The car purred to life and slid out seamlessly into the traffic, and she settled back against the seat and allowed herself to be pampered.

Soft music flowed around them, and as he drove they chatted about this and that. He was so easy to talk to, she thought, with his teasing sense of humour and his ready wit, but there was so much more to him, such depth and breadth and a wonderful human warmth that drew her like a moth to a flame.

Don't start having fantasies about him, she warned herself, but it was pointless. Every moment in his company she felt herself drawn closer to him, and by the time they arrived at his house she knew she was in deep trouble.

For the first time in her life, she realised, she was in serious danger of falling in love. Not lust, not a teenage crush or the hopeful dreams of a lonely young mother, but love.

And only a fool would allow herself to fall in love with a man who was so clearly out of reach.

CHAPTER FOUR

IT WAS a wonderful house. Snuggled into the side of a hill off a winding country lane, the old half-timbered barn looked out over the gently rolling farmland to the woods on the far side.

Autumn colour was just beginning to touch the leaves, and Cait guessed that in a few weeks the blaze of colour would be spectacular. In between, the land was freshly ploughed, the turned earth like rich, dark chocolate, and in the distance she could see a tractor moving slowly across a field, seagulls swooping and fluttering in its wake like the tail of a kite.

She breathed deeply of the fresh country air and thought of Josh and Milly stuck in the middle of London, surrounded by all those fumes, and she wanted to cry for them.

Owen opened the door and held out an arm to her, beckoning her inside with a smile. 'Come on in—dogs, get down!' he said, and the dogs subsided, wagging round them both and sniffing her with interest. 'They're just checking you out, they won't hurt you,' he told her, not that she needed reassuring. She guessed she was more in danger of being licked to death. 'This one's Daisy, the other one's Jess. Say hello nicely, girls.'

Cait looked at them, identical chocolate Labradors, and wondered how on earth he could tell the difference.

'Different collars,' he explained, reading her mind, and she laughed and patted them, introducing herself and trying to learn the difference, and then she straightened up and saw the interior of the barn, and fell in love all over again.

'Oh, wow,' she said softly, her breath almost taken away. They were in a lobby near one end, and through the open doorway she could see a wonderfully cosy sitting room at the end nearest her, and then beyond an open studwork partition the dining room soaring to the roof, with huge windows on both sides stretching up to the eaves.

A massive stove squatted between the two rooms, a gleaming stainless steel stovepipe emerging from the top of it and stretching up towards the roof. At the far end of the dining room two steps rose to the kitchen, with more open studwork to divide it from the central area.

'Come on in,' he said.

She followed Owen through the cosy and inviting sitting room into the central dining room, and tilting her head back she looked up into the great beamed vault of the roof. The ends were divided off with closed studwork, the beams still visible, so that over the kitchen and sitting room were two rooms, presumably bedrooms, and between them a walkway was suspended from the tie beams by steel rods, accessed by a sweeping spiral staircase in gleaming steel.

It was a fascinating mix of ancient and modern—sort of high tech meets country, Cait thought, and then she moved her head and caught a glimpse of the view through the wall of glass, and she was spellbound.

'Oh, it's gorgeous!' she said with feeling.

'You like it?' he asked, sounding curiously vulnerable. She turned to him in amazement.

'Like it? It's wonderful! Of course I like it!'

'Not everybody does. Bit rustic. Jill wouldn't have liked

it—she used to say she couldn't understand why anyone would want to live in a shed.'

Hence the vulnerability. Oh, yipes.

'Maybe it wasn't her kind of thing,' she said carefully, anxious not to criticise the dead woman. 'It might be a bit…informal for some tastes.'

Owen nodded. 'She liked order and everything in its place. We had a big Victorian house in the town before— formal and elegant and no surprises—and for all she loved them to bits, the dogs weren't allowed out of the kitchen and breakfast areas.'

'And now I suppose they sleep on your bed,' she teased.

He laughed softly. 'No. Just the settees. It's a bit hard to stop them when there isn't a door to close, but I don't care. It's not a showpiece, it's a home.'

'I think it's gorgeous,' she said, wondering how to ask him to show her round and unable to say the words. She didn't know him well enough, and it was such an intrusion.

'You want a guided tour?'

She pulled a wry face. 'I'm sorry. Is it so obvious?'

Owen laughed. 'Don't worry. I know what it's like. I love looking at other people's houses. It's so revealing.'

Thank goodness I didn't let him up into the flat this morning, then, she thought with a bubble of hysterical laughter threatening. Revealing wasn't in it. He would have run a mile!

He took her through the ground floor first, back past the front door in the lobby and through to a pair of bedrooms each with doors out to the garden and their own shower room just next to them. 'Josh has this bit of the house,' he explained, but it was self-evident in the posters and clutter and general abundance of teenage gear, even without all the things he'd taken away.

'What a good idea,' she said, regretting the smallness

of her flat. 'It must be more peaceful. Milly's music drives me potty.'

He laughed. 'Ditto. The house isn't very good at being soundproof with all the open studwork. This way I didn't have to listen to *his* dreadful choice in music.'

They retraced their footsteps back through the sitting room and dining room and into the kitchen. While Cait looked round enviously at all the cupboards and conjured with the very thought of having enough room for a central work island, he put the kettle on the Aga and gave her a quick glance at the pantry and utility room, then he led her up the staircase to the bedrooms.

'This is the spare room,' he said, taking her along the walkway to the one over the sitting room.

'Oh, it's huge!' Cait said, looking round at the four-poster bed nestled under the roof, with the window opposite so you could lie in bed in the morning and look at the woods and the fields and wallow in the beauty of it all.

'Why don't you sleep in here?' she asked, sticking her head round the door of the *en suite* bathroom. 'It's gorgeous.'

'I know. It's a lovely room and it's got a fabulous view, but I prefer the other one. It's over the Aga and it's warmer, and it's got a funny door. It just appeals to me.'

She followed him back down the walkway to the other room, and he pointed out the door that was cut along the top to fit the contours of the beam. She had to duck to clear the beam, and climb three little steps, and then they were in his bedroom.

The bed was huge, and yet it seemed scarcely big enough for the vast expanse of space. A row of doors in aged oak led to the little shower room, the loo and the walk-in wardrobe down one side, and on the other was a window criss-crossed with beams, looking out over the valley again.

Owen glanced round and rubbed his chin ruefully. 'I'm sorry, it's not exactly tidy. Mrs Poole doesn't arrive until eleven and I left in a bit of a hurry this morning, so I didn't make the bed.'

'Don't apologise—I didn't make mine, either,' she said with a laugh, but her eye was drawn to the tousled quilt and the dented pillow, and she felt a shiver of hot and cold run over her. Suddenly the enormous room seemed tiny and Owen seemed very, very close—scarily close, and extremely male.

I'm going to make a fool of myself, Cait thought, but then a noise caught her attention, a high-pitched whistle, and he turned towards the door.

'The kettle's boiling,' he said. 'Mind your head on the way out.'

'Why don't I go and take it off while you change?' she suggested, and he turned on the steps and bumped into her, reaching up to steady her.

Their eyes locked, and Cait couldn't breathe. Oh, lord, now what? she thought, but he seemed to pull himself together visibly. 'Good idea,' he said, and stepped back, knocking his head on a beam behind him.

He ducked and swore softly, and Cait made her escape down the stairs to the kitchen, stifling a chuckle.

The dogs were bracketing the Aga, and she stepped over them to remove the kettle. 'I hope you really are friendly,' she said, and they thumped their tails and grinned at her. 'I take it that's a yes.'

'Coffee's in the cupboard next to the Aga,' Owen called down. 'Instant or real—take your pick. There are teabags, too. The fridge is in the corner.'

'Thanks,' she called back, suddenly aware of how close

he was and what he was doing. Excitement tingled along her veins, and she tried not to think about him changing his clothes so very close to her. She could hear the odd clonk that was probably shoes coming off or going on, and drawers and doors opening and shutting, and the slight creak of the bed as he sat on it.

There had been a towel draped over the end of the bed, but she hadn't noticed any pyjamas lying around. Did that mean he slept naked? Heat shimmered over her skin, and she slapped her wrist.

'Cait, behave,' she told herself fiercely. 'It's none of your business.'

But she wanted it to be. For the first time in her adult life, she really, really wanted to develop a relationship with a man—this man, this funny, sensitive, generous man with eyes like molten toffee and lips she was aching to kiss...

Owen sat on the edge of the bed and sighed. He was going to make an idiot of himself over her, just because she was warm and gentle and funny and seemed totally unaware of how lovely she was.

He'd nearly kissed her when he'd turned on the steps and bumped into her, and her mouth had been just there in front of his, soft and slightly parted with surprise, and the longing had hit him like a thunderbolt.

Then he'd leapt out of the way and crowned himself on that beam, and she'd run down to the kitchen, no doubt splitting her sides laughing at him.

He rubbed the back of his head ruefully and sighed again. Damn. He had a bruise. Oh, well, it would serve him right—remind him not to make an idiot of himself. Or at least a worse idiot than he already had. He tugged on his jeans and a thick rugby shirt, pulled a sweater out of the drawer and put on his comfortable old shoes, then ran down to the kitchen.

'What did you make?' he asked, but she just smiled that lovely wide smile and shook her head, and heat slammed through him.

'Nothing. I didn't know what you'd want. I'll make it now, if you like.'

Suddenly the kitchen seemed terribly small and intimate, and with nobody else around to dilute the atmosphere he could hardly breathe. Plus any minute now Mrs Poole would be here, and he couldn't cope with her insatiable curiosity. 'Let's go out,' he suggested rapidly. 'We'll get coffee somewhere—unless you'd rather not?'

She shook her head again. 'I don't mind. Whatever.'

'We'll go out,' he said, more firmly, and headed for the door.

Was it something she'd said? Owen seemed preoccupied and uncomfortable, and Cait wondered if it was because she'd said she liked the barn and reminded him about his wife.

Had he taken her remarks as a criticism? Surely not—she'd only said she liked the house, but maybe he felt guilty because he liked it, too, and if Jill wouldn't have done—oh, it was hopeless. She couldn't work it out, she didn't know enough about him, so she sat quietly beside him as he drove across to the coast, and they walked along the front at Aldeburgh in the keen October wind, and when their fingers and noses were frozen they took refuge in a hotel bar for coffee.

He seemed more relaxed now, and so she found herself able to relax and enjoy his company. He was very easy to talk to, and after a while she found herself talking about Milly.

'I was so worried about how she'd cope, but she seems to be having loads of fun. Partying till dawn, by all accounts. I don't know, I never had so much fun when I was her age—well, of course I didn't, because I had her running around underfoot all day and night.'

He studied her thoughtfully over his coffee cup. 'You must have been very young when you had her,' he said in a gentle voice totally devoid of criticism. 'It must have been hard.'

'It was. I was seventeen—just. My parents were in the throes of splitting up, my boyfriend's parents had split up—we were in the same boat, really, and I suppose we just turned to each other for comfort. Anyway, when I found I was pregnant my parents went off at the deep end and threw me out, and he was sent away to sixth-form college, and that was the end of that. He wrote for a while, but he never sees her and he's living abroad so I don't get any financial help from him. I never have had—well, that's not quite true. He sent her a cheque for a hundred pounds for her eighteenth birthday and she gave it to me because she said she didn't want it and my car needed servicing.'

Oh, dear. She hadn't meant to tell him that, to let him know how close she came to the wire in a bad month, or what a knife-edge they lived on. She had no sickness insurance, so if she had to have time off—well, she couldn't, and she'd always managed to struggle downstairs to the shop no matter how bad she'd felt, and luckily she'd been reasonably well.

The threat was there, though, and it worried her, but it wasn't Owen's business, and he didn't need to know.

'I thought we were young, at twenty-one,' he told her, and she did a quick calculation that made him thirty-nine, just four years older than her. 'How on earth did you manage? At least we had help from our parents, and we had each other. It must have been a nightmare on your own.'

Cait nodded agreement. 'I stayed with a friend until the baby was born, then the council gave me a flat, and I started doing alterations and making clothes for people. I picked up an old sewing machine and someone gave me an overlocker that didn't work, and I got it mended for a few pounds and used it for years.'

'So what gave you the idea of the shop?' he asked curiously, and she smiled.

'Money. A friend asked me to make her a ball gown, and said she'd gone to a hire shop and the cost was outrageous. I made the dress for less than the cost of the hire, and she said it was one of the nicest at the ball. Some of her friends came to me, and then they didn't want them again and started to swap, and I thought, if I had a hire shop, I could appeal to a wider market.'

'So you opened the shop.'

'Yes—and I've been there ever since. It's been wonderful, because living overhead I could work in the holidays without compromising Milly's safety, and it was within walking distance of her school and friends without being in a town centre, and it's got parking outside for customers—it's perfect.'

'Don't you get cabin fever?' he asked with a little smile, and she laughed.

'Every day. Still, I do what I have to do, and it's a lovely little place. I've got friends who drop in for coffee, and one of them will mind the shop for me if we go on holiday or go out for the day. It's OK.'

'I think you're amazing,' he said softly. 'To do what you've done for Milly, to hold the two of you together from the age of seventeen, to give her the chances you've given her with so little help—that takes a special kind of woman. I take my hat off to you. You're one gutsy lady, Cait Cooper, and you have my unqualified admiration.'

Soft colour flooded her cheeks, and she looked down, embarrassed and yet deeply touched by his praise. 'Thank you,' she said, her voice slightly choked, and he set his cup down and stood up.

'Come on, let's go back to the car and find somewhere for lunch—unless you want to go back?'

No, of course she didn't want to go back. She never wanted to go back.

'I have an essay waiting for me, remember, but I dare say it'll keep that long.'

His smile was warm and coaxing. 'I'm sure it will. Come on. You've spent eighteen years towing the line. It's time to cut yourself a little slack.'

'But the evening class was supposed to be for me!'

'It's work!' he said disgustedly. 'You need to learn how to play.'

'That's easy to say, but I don't have a playmate,' she said without thinking.

'Oh, yes, you do,' he said, and he sounded almost excited. 'I've been working too hard as well. Why don't we have our own Freshers' week? The kids are having all this fun—how about us? We could do all the things they're doing—the pub crawl, the balls, the floating restaurant, the fancy-dress party—all of it. What do you say?'

She laughed. 'You're crazy,' she told him, half-tempted. 'You're absolutely nuts.'

'No, I'm not. I had to grow up too fast, too soon, just like you. Now Jill's gone and Josh is away, and there's nothing left. It's time to start again, Cait—for both of us. Let's go for it.'

She looked up into his amazing liquid toffee eyes and was lost.

'OK,' she said slowly, and wondered just how long it would be before he broke her heart.

CHAPTER FIVE

'So, WHAT are we doing tonight?'

Cait laughed and shook her head at Owen. 'No. I have to go to my evening class.'

'I thought we'd discussed this?' he said with a grin, but she shook her head again.

'No, you told me it was work, and it *is* work, but it's work for me and not just for the coffers, and that's different. Anyway, I'm enjoying it,' she lied. 'Another night.'

'Tomorrow?'

'I've got to finish that wedding dress. It'll take me all week.'

'Friday, then,' he said promptly. 'We'll start on Friday—and no more excuses.'

She couldn't help her answering smile. 'No excuses,' she agreed.

There was a pause, and then his hands came up and cupped her shoulders, and he lowered his mouth to hers— just briefly, the merest brush of his lips, but it sent fire skittering through her body. He lifted his head, and his eyes were molten gold.

'I'll see you on Friday,' he said huskily, and turned away, leaving her propping herself up against the shop door because her legs had simply stopped working and if she moved she'd fall over.

He drove away with a lift of his hand, and she watched him go before turning and letting herself inside. She went up to the flat on her rubbery legs and looked around, and thought what a dismal and tired little place it was after his barn.

She'd done her best with it, making curtains and loose covers to brighten it up, but when you were starting from something pretty ordinary it was hard to make it special. Perhaps it was time to decorate it—go for a new look perhaps?

Or perhaps it was time to write her essay before her evening class started in three hours!

Owen phoned on Friday at five to ask what time he should pick her up, and told her to wear something nice.

'What are we doing?' she asked.

'Milly and Josh are going to a toga party,' he told her 'I thought we could do a modern version.'

'Of a *toga party*!' she all but shrieked.

His chuckle came down the line. 'Don't worry, I'm not going to strut around doing Charlton Heston impressions. I thought we could go to that floating Italian restaurant for dinner.'

'What's that got to do with togas?' she asked warily.

'Nothing. Modern-day Romans.'

She felt her shoulders drop with relief. 'So, how smart? she asked, mentally scanning her rather slight wardrobe.

'How smart do you want to be? It can be quite dressy there.'

She'd drawn a blank on her own wardrobe, but she did have a rather lovely little black dress in stock downstairs—

'Dressy will do fine,' she said, suddenly decided. 'Pick me up whenever. Do you have a reservation?'

'No—I'll make one and call you back.'

By the time he rang, she'd dashed down to the shop, rummaged through the rails and found the dress. She'd just slipped it over her head when the phone rang, and she picked it up and said 'Hello?' a little breathlessly.

'Been running?' Owen teased, and she laughed and put her hand over her chest to steady her pounding heart that owed much more to the sound of his voice than the exercise.

'I was trying on a dress,' she told him, turning this way and that and looking at it in the mirror. Good grief. She really ought to put on proper clothes more often, they made her feel wonderful!

'How does seven sound?' he asked, and she had to bite her tongue so she didn't tell him it was too soon. She had to shower and wash her hair, and inevitably it would refuse to behave and so she'd have to put it up, and she had no idea where her make-up was or if Milly had 'borrowed' it and taken it to London—

'Seven's fine,' she lied, and then ran round like a headless chicken, panicking.

Still, she was ready at a quarter to seven and had to force herself to sit still and not haunt the window looking out for him. Even so, she saw the sweep of Owen's headlights as he came into the little square, and she grabbed her coat and bag and ran down the stairs, locking the shop door behind her just as he stepped out of the car.

She stopped in her tracks. He was wearing a dinner jacket and black bow-tie on crisp white, and she could see the gleam of his shoes from where she was standing. He looked gorgeous, and her heart began to hammer.

'Hi, there,' she said with a dredged-up smile, and he smiled back a little distractedly.

His eyes scanned her and then came back and locked with hers. 'You look beautiful,' he said softly, and she felt the colour rise in her cheeks and take the place of the blusher she hadn't been able to find.

No matter. If he kept paying her compliments like that, she'd never need it again!

Cait was stunning. All week long she'd been on his mind, her courage and her determination astounding him. Most girls in her situation would have taken the easy way out, but she'd hung on and had had her baby and raised a young woman to be proud of, at the cost of her own youth.

Well, he couldn't give her back her youth, but he could give it his best shot, and he had spent the week dreaming up a whole plethora of things he could do with her. He'd jotted down a list of things Josh had told him they'd done, and he'd racked his brains to find adult equivalents.

He'd come up with something for most of them, but he'd drawn a blank on a respectable and acceptable version of licking vodka jelly off each other! He thought maybe he'd save that one for later on.

Much later on!

In the meantime, he was faced with the most beautiful woman he'd seen in a long, long time, and he didn't know if it was because she was classically beautiful, which she wasn't, or if it was because of the glow in her skin and the light in her eyes and the way her mouth trembled in that shy smile when he complimented her.

There was a staggering innocence about her, a virginal quality that brought out the chivalrous hero in him and subdued the caveman who wanted nothing more than to drag her off to his cave and make babies with her. Even so, standing here looking at her in that incredibly sexy little dress, he could hear the caveman roaring with frustration.

Down, boy, he cautioned. Allowing himself the privilege of dropping a light kiss on her cheek, he ushered her into the car and drove her to the docks. He parked near the restaurant at the back of a friend's gallery, and they strolled arm in arm along the water's edge to the converted barge that housed their destination.

Their table was by a window, and they could see the lights of the converted maltings opposite reflected in the ruffled water. There was soft music playing in the background, and everything they said seemed wittier than usual.

Finally, though, their meal was over and they'd drained the coffee-pot, and she looked round the nearly empty restaurant and smiled sadly. 'I suppose we ought to go,' she said, and she sounded regretful.

Owen hailed the waiter, unwilling to let the evening end, and after paying the bill he drew her to her feet. 'Come on,' he said, 'the night's still young.'

'It's nearly eleven!' she protested.

'Perfect. We're going clubbing.'

'Clubbing!' she squeaked, making the other diners look up in surprise. She blushed and he hid a smile and put his arm round her shoulders and led her down to the lower deck and out onto the dockside.

'Clubbing,' he repeated. 'It's over-thirties night, and we both qualify. Come on, you were complaining you hadn't lived.'

'I was?' she said with a laugh. 'I haven't been clubbing for about fifteen years!'

'Well, it's high time you did.' Owen turned her collar up against the cold, tucked her under his arm and they strolled down the dock to the centre of the local nightspots. The music was loud, the beat heavy and insistent, and he drew her into his arms on the dance floor and felt the caveman roar to life.

Cait moved like a dancer, her body fluid and supple, and her head found a natural resting place in the hollow of his shoulder. He forced the caveman back under control, and cradled her against his chest. She was too sweet and innocent to deal with the raging need that was surfacing in him, and he kept it firmly at bay, denying his urge to rock her hard against his aching body.

The tempo changed, to his relief, and became faster, and he released her and instead had to endure the torture of watching her body move to the music. Then it slowed again, and she went back into his arms, and he gave in and held her close, and for an instant he felt her stiffen with shock as she became aware of his arousal.

Then she moved closer, her body relaxing against him, and he rested his head against hers and let out his breath in a long, ragged sigh. His lips brushed her neck, and it arched for him instinctively. No, he told himself. Don't start what you can't finish.

An ache of longing racked his body, and he closed his eyes against it and swayed with her to the music, content for now just to hold her. Oh, his body wasn't content, but his head was, and it was his head he had to listen to.

He wasn't ready yet for more, and nor was she, at least not with him.

Not yet, and maybe not ever.

She'd had fun, more fun than she'd had for years, and in the way Owen had he'd made her feel really special, but inevitably it had to come to an end. He took her home at a little after one, because she had to open the shop next morning and she needed a few hours' sleep.

He pulled up outside, and Cait hesitated before opening the car door. 'Would you like a coffee?' she asked, but he shook his head.

'No. I don't think so. It's late, and you've got to get up.'

His hand reached out and cupped her cheek gently, and

drew her towards him. 'Thank you for a wonderful evening,' he murmured softly, and then his lips claimed hers in a chaste, tender kiss that nevertheless made her bones melt and her breath jam in her throat.

Then, all too soon, he drew away and got out of the car, opening the door for her and seeing her in, brushing her lips one last time before he turned on his heel and walked back to the car.

She nearly ran after him, but her pride stopped her at the last moment, and instead she stood there on legs that seemed permanently useless these days and watched him go, then closed the door and locked it.

It had been a wonderful evening, he was right, and she hadn't wanted it to end. He had, though, or he would have taken her up on her offer of coffee. Perhaps it was just as well. It wasn't really coffee that she'd wanted, but just more time with him, and maybe that would have been too dangerous.

She went upstairs and found a message on the answering machine from Milly. She sounded puzzled that her mother had been out, and Cait sighed and took off the dress and hung it up. She'd get it dry-cleaned and put it back in stock—or maybe she'd keep it. She'd felt wonderful in it tonight, elegant and sexy and beautiful.

Yes, she'd keep it.

She looked at her watch. It was too late to ring Milly now. She'd phone her in the morning. It didn't sound urgent, but the mother in her suffered a pang of guilt because she hadn't been there.

What if it had been urgent? What if Milly *had* needed her?

The phone rang, and she answered it instantly.

'I just wanted to say goodnight,' Owen said, his voice soft and slightly gruff. 'I didn't wake you, did I?'

'No—no, you didn't wake me, I haven't gone to bed yet. I missed a call from Milly,' she told him, and heard him sigh.

'I'm sorry. Was it urgent?'

'Didn't sound it, but you can't always tell. I don't know. Tell me I'm being silly.'

'I can't. I missed a call from Josh. I'll message him on his mobile—want me to message Emily?'

So that she knew her mother had been with Owen? Not likely! The inquisition would be unparalleled. 'Don't worry, I'll ring her tomorrow. Owen?'

'What?'

'Have you told Josh we've...seen each other?' she asked, not sure how to put it.

He sighed. 'No. I didn't know what to say, or even if there was anything to tell him. There hasn't been anyone since Jill—I don't know how he'll react. I'll tell him myself maybe, face to face. What about you? Have you told Milly?'

'No. I don't...have a social life. Well, not this sort, anyway,' she added, feeling the colour climb her cheeks.

'Cait, we haven't done anything wrong,' he said gently, and she sighed.

'I know. It's just—'

'I know. Don't worry—maybe we'll cross that bridge together later, if we get to that point. In the meantime, tell her something else—tell her you went to the supermarket,' he suggested, and she laughed.

'It wouldn't be the first time,' she told him. 'Since it started opening twenty-four hours a day, I've often been in the middle of the night. It's sometimes the only time left. I just hate lying to her.'

'So tell her you went out with a friend. It's not so far from the truth, is it?'

He sounded almost wistful, and Cait smiled sadly. 'No. No, it's not far from the truth at all. I'll tell her that.'

'Good. And I'll see you tonight.'

'Tonight?' she echoed, her heart racing. He hadn't mentioned another date, and she'd been feeling a little rejected. How silly.

'Or tomorrow, whatever you want to call it. Saturday night. Wear something more casual, and don't eat. I'll see you at seven-thirty.'

'I'll look forward to it,' she said, wondering if he could hear the eagerness she knew must be in her voice. 'And...Owen?'

'Mmm?'

'Thank you for tonight.'

There was a tiny hesitation, then he said softly, 'You're welcome, sweetheart. It was my pleasure. See you soon. Sleep well.'

She replaced the phone regretfully, stripped off her make-up and climbed into bed in her serviceable old night-shirt. Her body was still humming from the contact with his as they'd danced, and just the memory made her ache for more.

He'd obviously been affected by their dance, too, and had been unable to disguise his reaction, but unlike the average man he'd made no move to pursue that interest or push her into anything she wasn't ready for.

Still, he'd proved over and over again that he was more than an average man, and he was a lot more mature than the last man to take an interest in her. Still, that had been fifteen or so years ago, and that thoroughly average experience had been enough to put her off for life.

Until Owen.

She wondered what he'd got planned for them that night. Goodness knows. He'd given her no clues on the phone, apart from telling her not to eat and to dress casually. Still, she didn't care. Just being with him was enough.

Cait snuggled down under the quilt, closed her eyes and fell instantly asleep, happier than she'd been for years.

CHAPTER SIX

'A PUB crawl!'

Owen laughed, his eyes crinkling with humour and his lips twitching. 'Yes, a pub crawl. Are you doing anything early tomorrow?'

Cait shook her head, wondering what was in store for her that he needed to ask that. 'No. Nothing—well, I was going to sort stock at some point. Why, won't I be well enough?'

He laughed again. 'Of course you will! I'm not going to get you legless, sweetheart. I was just going to suggest you bring some overnight things, then we can go by taxi and I can get in the spirit of it, too—or we can do that and I can get the taxi to run you back. It's up to you. No strings. I just thought it might be rather nice to have our own sleep-over party.'

She hesitated for a moment, troubled because she still hadn't been able to get hold of Milly on the phone, but then she surrendered with a smile. 'OK. I'll get some things together. Come on up—it's tidy for once. I cleaned up in your honour.'

'I'd better come and make it worthwhile, then, hadn't I?' he said with a grin, and followed her up the stairs.

She turned to him at the top. 'It's not like yours,' she warned him.

Owen caught her hands and held them lightly, staring down into her eyes, his face serious now. 'I didn't expect it to be, Cait. Stop worrying. You know I'm proud of all you've achieved. I'm not interested in judging you.'

She felt tears welling in her eyes, and turned away. 'Don't be silly. Come in.'

He followed her, looking round with interest. She'd thought he'd probably sit politely down, but he didn't. He prowled, fingering things, looking at her little treasures—clay models Milly had made at kindergarten, a framed Mother's Day card ditto, a funny little knitted cat that was meant to be Bagpuss.

He smiled indulgently as he examined them, and she could tell that he had a similar set of treasures collected over the years. He was a sentimental man, and she wondered how he had coped with Jill's death and if it still haunted him.

Certainly he still wore his wedding ring, and she wondered if he was ready for another relationship or if he really was just offering her friendship with no strings attached, just as he'd said.

'I won't be long. Sit down,' she suggested hopefully, but he just smiled and said he was all right and carried on prowling.

Cait came back a few minutes later after a hunt for a decent nightdress, to find him on the lumpy old sofa with Bagpuss shedding hair all over his dark trousers.

'Oh, no, look what's she's done!' she exclaimed, and handed Owen the clothes brush. There was no way she was brushing down his lap!

'OK?' he asked after a few vigorous strokes, and she nodded.

'You'll do. Sorry about that—you're a bad cat, Bagpuss! Come on, I'll feed you. You'd better have enough to last tomorrow morning, if Owen's going to lead me astray,' she said to the cat, who just purred and wound herself around Cait's legs.

Owen was chuckling.

'What?' she said.

'Me, leading you astray. As if I would,' he murmured, and winked at her.

She sighed inwardly. Unfortunately she didn't think there was the slightest chance of him leading her astray, despite the wink. He was far too much of a gentleman, and she had a sickening feeling that he wanted much less from her than she wanted to give.

But, then, she was a desperate, lonely old maid.

Not that she'd have to be desperate to take an interest in him. He was enough to tempt a saint, and she'd lost any right to that office years ago. Oh, rats.

'Right, I'm ready,' she said, throwing the cat an extra measure of dry food and making a friend for life of her.

She flicked off lights, left the landing light on and ran down the stairs with Owen following her, her overnight bag firmly in his hand after he'd removed it from her.

Ever the gentleman.

She shut the door from the stairwell to the shop, locked it and then set the shop alarm on the way out of the door.

'Is there any risk of a break-in?' he asked her, and she shrugged.

'I don't know. I didn't want to take any chances, so I tend to set the alarm if I'm out for a long time—although they say most burglaries happen when you've gone to fetch a child from school or nipped to the shop, don't they?'

'Something like that. We were burgled in town while we were at home, for goodness' sake—just because we left the window open in the sitting room when we'd gone out into the garden. They came in through the bay window in full view of the street, and nobody saw a thing.'

She thought how she'd feel, and shuddered. 'It must have been awful. Did they take much?'

He gave a slow shake of his head. 'Not really. They broke something irreplaceable, though, a cup Josh had made for Jill at school. That was the worst thing. Nothing else seemed to matter by comparison.'

He opened the car door for her, and she looked up and caught a glimpse of pain in his eyes, and knew she'd been right. He was a man who valued little things, who knew the importance of tiny gestures and acts of kindness, and she felt her throat swell with emotion so that she could hardly swallow.

By the time he was behind the wheel she'd got herself together again, and he shot her a smile that didn't quite reach his eyes. 'OK?' he said, and she nodded, not quite able to trust her voice.

'Yes, I'm OK,' she managed after a moment, then changed the subject. 'So, where are we starting this pub crawl?' she asked brightly.

'Oh, in Audley. I've got a taxi coming for us at eight-fifteen.'

'Such extravagance,' she teased, and he shrugged.

'You could drive, if you like, but it rather defeats the object.'

'So it does,' she agreed. 'So, which pub first and why?'

'The Dirty Duck—they have a brilliant starter menu.'

'Starter menu?' she said, puzzled.

He shot her a grin. 'Oh, yes. You didn't think we were going to go to all these pubs and just drink, did you?'

She had—well, she'd imagined he'd told her not to eat so he could feed her, not so she'd get drunk quicker, but she had no real idea what he'd got in mind.

It turned out to be a culinary guided tour. They had chopped mushrooms and smoky bacon on toast in the Dirty Duck, washed down with a glass of something de-licious from their wine cellar, followed by a brisk walk across town to the Wagon and Horses for a wonderful pot roast with the most fabulous vegetables and a glass of vintage claret, then on to the Bell for the wickedest chocolate mousse she'd ever tasted in her life, sitting on a puddle of Grand Marnier and topped with the creamiest cream and a fanned strawberry garnish, with a glass of wonderfully mellow muscat to sip alongside it.

'That,' she told him as she scraped the last tiny bit of chocolate mousse from the dish and levelled her spoon at him, 'was not your average pub crawl.'

Owen chuckled. 'I thought you'd never been on one?' he said.

'That doesn't mean I don't know what they're like,' she pointed out, 'and that wasn't it.' She sat back, still licking her lips, and sighed hugely. 'That was...' She trailed to a halt, lost for words, and he gave a low chuckle.

'That good, eh?'

'Absolutely. Remind me never to cook for you—it's just underlined how useless I really am.'

He chuckled again and poured the last dribble of muscat into her glass. 'Come on, drink up, we've got to have the next course.'

Cait stared at him in open-mouthed amazement. 'Next course?' she squeaked, and he nodded.

'Yup—Irish coffee and after-dinner mints by the fire at my house. The taxi'll be outside in a moment. Are you ready?'

She nodded, a little dazed. 'Yes, I'm ready. I don't know if I can stand, but I'm ready.' She smiled at him, wondering if she looked and sounded as merry as she felt, and remembered his promise not to get her legless.

Well, it wasn't exactly a promise, which was just as well since he probably had no idea what a cheap drunk she was.

One sip and she was away usually, and tonight she'd had three glasses.

Oops.

Oh, well, in for a penny…

She drained her glass and stood up, managing not to fall over while he helped her into her coat, and then the taxi whisked them back out into the velvet darkness of the countryside and she leant on his arm in the back and sighed contentedly.

'OK?'

'Mmm.' She felt too lazy to speak, and didn't argue when he eased his arm out from behind her and wrapped it round her shoulders, shifting so that her head came to rest on his chest and her arm just naturally snuggled round his waist. 'Mmm,' she said again, and closed her eyes. It felt so good…

She was asleep by the time they got back to his house, and he woke her gently. 'Cait? We're back.'

She sat up sleepily, and he got out of the taxi and paid the driver, then went round and helped her out.

'Come on, sleepyhead,' he said gently, and she looked up at him as the clouds parted, her face silvered with moonlight, and smiled mistily.

'Sorry—I'm not used to drinking so much,' she told him, as if he hadn't already realised that. 'It just knocks me out.'

'You can't go to sleep yet, we've still got to have the coffee and liqueur phase of the meal,' he reminded her.

'Just coffee,' she told him, sounding just a fraction tipsy, and he felt a twinge of guilt. Hopefully she wouldn't feel too hungover the next day.

'Come on,' he coaxed, and led her into the house and settled her in the corner of the settee nearest the fire.

The dogs greeted them with enthusiastic wagging, and

he let them out for a run and gave them a biscuit while he made the coffee.

He passed on the Irish whiskey. Cait certainly didn't need it and he wasn't sure he did, either. The last thing he wanted was to drink so much that he woke up tomorrow not knowing what he'd done, if anything, and he needed all his wits about him with her looking so soft and warm and sleepy.

Owen sat down on the other side of the fireplace, well away from temptation, and pushed the coffee towards Cait across the low table.

'Hey, sleepyhead,' he said, and she cracked an eye open.

'You talking to me?' she asked, and he nodded.

'I am. Your coffee's there.'

'Laced?'

He shook his head. 'No. Not laced. I thought we'd probably both had enough.'

She sat forwards and kicked off her shoes, picked up her coffee and snuggled back into the corner with her feet tucked under her bottom and her nose buried in the mug.

'Mmm,' she said appreciatively, and he smiled and leant back, stretching out his legs in front of him and indulging his senses.

A warm fire, a comfortable chair, good coffee—and a beautiful woman to look at. What more could a man want?

To take her to bed and make long, slow, lazy love to her, he thought, and swore silently. Ain't ever gonna happen, he told himself. Down, boy. You promised.

He snagged a handful of chocolate mint sticks and nudged the stereo remote control, and soft music poured over them, lazy and romantic. They stayed there like that for ages, long after the coffee was finished and the fire had died down and the CD had played out, and then he stood up and drew her to her feet.

'Come on, let's get you to bed. You look wiped.'

'You said you weren't going to get me legless,' she teased, and stumbled slightly against him.

'Hopeless creature. You didn't tell me you had no head at all for it.'

'Of course I haven't! I'll have you know I'm a model of propriety,' she said, and spoilt it by giggling.

Owen gave up. Scooping her into his arms, he carried her up the stairs and along the walkway to her room, then set her gently down on her feet in the doorway. Her bag was there, all ready for her, and he thought she could probably manage to get herself ready for bed. If she couldn't, well, she'd sleep as she was, because there was no way he trusted himself with her, not when she was so deliciously defenceless.

He reached out a hand and cupped Cait's cheek, and the moonlight streaming through the window beside him gleamed dully on the worn gold of his wedding ring.

He looked at it in surprise. He hadn't even thought about it for a while, but now it seemed out of place, somehow disloyal to both Jill and Cait. And if anything could have reminded him of his responsibilities, that was it.

He dropped his hand to his side and gave her a crooked smile.

'Goodnight, sweetheart,' he murmured. 'Sleep well.'

His lips brushed hers lightly, and he turned and left her standing there in the doorway. He closed his door firmly, sat down on the edge of the bed and picked up the photo of Jill that sat on the bedside table.

Odd, how he could hardly remember her now after all the time they'd been together. He could still hear her voice sometimes in things Josh said, but he found it increasingly hard to remember her face.

Four years, he thought. Just a short while, and yet it felt like a lifetime.

He could hear Cait moving around in her room at the other end of the walkway, and he wished it was a draw-bridge that he could pull up, to keep them both safe from each other.

He put the photo of Jill back on the bedside table to watch over him and keep him in order, and then he took off his clothes, crawled under the quilt and lay listening to the small sounds from Cait's room until the house was quiet.

Then he fell into a restless sleep, and dreamed of her...

CHAPTER SEVEN

CAIT woke to sun streaming in and a pounding headache.

'Oh, no,' she groaned, and slid under the quilt, shutting out the light. Better, but not a lot. Oh, heck.

'Serves you right,' she told herself a while later when the little men had put their hammers down and seemed to be taking a tea-break. 'You know you can't drink.'

She heard a firm tread on the walkway and scraped up the mental energy to wonder just how much of a fright she looked. She'd taken her make-up off the night before, but without fail a trace of mascara would remain and work its way down her cheeks in the night, giving her panda eyes.

Her hair was on end, her head was thumping again and the last thing she wanted to do was put on a cheerful face. She decided not to bother. It was, after all, his fault.

After a gentle knock, Owen popped his head round the door. 'Hello, sleepyhead,' he said softly, and she twitched the quilt down and looked blearily at him across the room.

'Hello yourself,' she growled. 'You're looking disgustingly chipper.'

He smiled just a touch smugly. 'How's the head?'

'Grim. How's yours?'

'Fine,' he said, and finally had the grace to look apologetic. 'I've brought you tea, if you fancy it.'

Cait slid carefully up the bed, dragging the quilt after her, and tucked it firmly under her armpits. 'I always fancy tea,' she told him, and rested her head gently back against the high wooden headboard with a groan.

'Sit up,' he told her, and tucked another pillow behind her shoulders for her sore head to rest on. 'How's that?'

'Lovely,' she croaked, and reached for the tea. The mug arrived in her fingers, and she buried her nose in it and sipped cautiously. 'Oh, gorgeous,' she mumbled, and worked her way steadily down it.

By the time she'd finished the second cup, the little men were just tapping gently and she thought she might survive the day. Owen, bless his heart, was mercifully silent, just sitting by the window on a comfy chair sipping tea and staring out over the valley.

He looked across at her and smiled. 'Better?'

'Much, thank you,' she said with feeling. Putting the cup down, she snuggled the covers up round her shoulders and sighed. 'I can't believe I'm hungover,' she said disgustedly, and he chuckled.

'It was probably the muscat. It's wickedly strong.'

'It was perfect with the chocolate mousse—which incidentally had a good slug of liqueur in it. I forgot to count that.'

'Ah, yes, the chocolate mousse. I should have warned you. I've had it before—it's enough to put you over the limit without anything else, just about.'

'To be fair, I can get drunk on my neighbour's sherry-flavour trifle,' she said drily, and he chuckled again. She gave him a sour look. 'You're in a very good mood,' she said crossly.

One brow kicked up. 'Do I take it you aren't a morning person, sweetheart?' he said with an almost straight face, and she threw a pillow at him.

Owen caught it and threw it back, and she buried her face in it and rolled over onto her side, groaning. 'What time is it?' she asked through the pillow.

'If you just said what I think you did, it's eleven thirty.'

She dropped the pillow and sat up. 'What!' she squawked. 'It can't be!'

'It is. Why, should you be somewhere?'

Cait shook her head—not a wise move—and groaned.

'You need some breakfast and some fresh air, probably in the reverse order. Why don't you have a quick shower and we'll take the dogs for a little stroll down to the river, then come back and have a good hearty breakfast?'

'Go away,' she said very clearly, and fell back into the pillows with a groan.

He was utterly heartless, she decided later when she'd calmed down a bit. He smiled a barracuda smile, leant over and plucked the quilt off her in one easy movement, walking out of the room with it and dropping it over the banisters.

'I'll see you downstairs in five minutes,' he said, and she hurled a pillow at his head.

He ducked back out of the way, and she heard his chuckle echo down the stairs and into the kitchen.

Brute, she thought, lying back against the remaining pillow and wishing she could die. All the pillow-hurling had got the little men back from their tea-break, and she gave up the unequal struggle and slid off the bed, went into the bathroom and turned on the power shower and nearly blasted her skin off.

She felt better, irritatingly, but she had to concede the point. Maybe he'd be right about the fresh air and breakfast as well.

How sickening!

It was a beautiful day. They walked the dogs down through the fields and across the little bridge over the river, and then through the woods on the far side before coming back.

It was quiet and peaceful, with nothing to disturb them but the song of the birds and the rustle of squirrels in the trees. There was a stile to climb over, and Owen helped Cait down and then somehow forgot to let go of her so that they strolled back hand in hand, and she magnanimously forgave him for her hangover—even though it had really been her own fault.

'I'm sorry I was crabby,' she said as they got back to the house, and he turned her into his arms and kissed the tip of her nose and smiled.

'I forgive you. You were quite entertaining.'

She closed her eyes and counted to ten, but while they were shut he kissed her again, only on the lips this time, and she forgot to breathe—forgot everything, including how far out of her league he was and all the other reasons this might be a bad idea, and she went up on tiptoe and kissed him right back.

After a while he lifted his head and she sank down onto her heels again and rocked back and looked up at him, slightly dazed.

'Breakfast,' he said, his voice gruff, and she nodded and followed him in, her heart pounding.

Nobody had ever kissed her like that. Nobody. Ever. Not in thirty-five and a half years.

And all he could talk about was breakfast!

Owen took her back to her flat at three, and once again Milly had tried to phone—the night before, and twice during the morning.

'Get out of that,' she said with a sigh, and dropped into the armchair by the phone. She punched in the number, crossed her fingers and forced a smile into her voice.

'Hi, darling, how are you?' she asked brightly.

'Worried to death. Where have you *been*?'

'Sorry, sweetheart, I should have told you. I went out for a drink last night and then we went back for coffee and it was late so I stayed over. What's the matter? Is anything wrong?'

'No,' Milly said slowly. Damn. Cait could hear the cogs working. 'Who were you out with?'

What now? A direct lie, or the truth, when Owen hadn't told Josh yet?

'Nobody you know,' she said noncommittally.

'A man? Hey, Ma, have you got a man, after all this time? Amazing! Tell me all! What's he like?'

'I didn't say it was a man.'

'You didn't have to. It's in your voice, you sound different.' A slight pause, then, 'Did you say you stayed over?'

Cait closed her eyes and prayed for the ground to open up. 'Nothing happened,' she said truthfully. 'I stayed in the spare room. Alone. All night.'

'Oh.' Silence while her daughter digested this, then with the resilience of youth she moved on. 'Anyway, why I was ringing was, there's this ball coming up—the Hall Freshers' Ball? It's next weekend, and I don't have a dress with me, and I don't suppose there's any way you could throw something together and send it down, is there?'

'What, post it?' she said, wondering what on earth it would cost and if it would arrive, but Milly was way ahead of her with it all worked out.

'No, not post it,' she said. 'Josh's dad is coming down next Friday for a conference. If I give you his address, you could let him have it, and he could bring it down!'

Da-dah!

Cait waited for a white rabbit to pop out of the end of the phone. So easy. Just make me a dress, give it to a man you don't know—hah—to bring me, and hey presto! Madam could go to the ball.

Never mind that her mother might not have time to do it!

'What sort of dress?' she asked, actually only too glad to get Milly permanently off the subject of her sleep-over party with Owen.

'Oh, you know—something a bit like that gold one but less bad.'

Cait nearly choked. 'The gold one?' she squeaked.

'Yes, you know, that strappy thing.'

Straps was all it was. It was the one Owen had jokingly pulled out, and there was no way her darling little daughter was going anywhere in a creation like that!

'I've sold it,' she lied, but Milly snorted.

'You just don't want me wearing a slapper's dress,' she retorted, hitting the nail on the head, and Cait sighed.

'Why on earth would you want to?' she asked with a touch of desperation. 'Anyway, I don't have time. How about a nice simple halter-neck dress with a pouffy underskirt and a stole? Or something slinky—a crêpe cut on the cross, or a shot-silk bodice and a black skirt? There are lots of them around this year—'

'Mum, you're boring! I'm not thirty! I want something young!'

'So go and buy one!' she suggested, but Milly sighed unhappily and so they started again, renegotiating until they came to some kind of compromise.

'So, when will you start it?' she asked, and Cait rolled her eyes.

'I'll look through my fabric stocks now. I'm sure I've got something that will do. I just hope it fits, because there's nothing I can do about it if it doesn't.'

'It'll fit,' her daughter said with confidence, and Cait

hoped she was right. Still, she could set up the model to Milly's size, which would help.

'OK, darling, I'll see what I can do.'

'Right—and, Ma? You have fun, OK? You deserve it. You've given up enough for me. It's time you had some fun. Go for it.'

Oh, lord. Cait felt her heart rising up in her throat and threatening to choke her. 'Thanks, darling,' she said unsteadily, and after a few maternal warnings about sex and drugs and alcohol and not working hard enough, she put down the phone and sat back, her mind whirling.

Go for it?

Really?

Still, why not? As Milly had pointed out, she'd given up enough. It was time for her—and she ought to take advantage of every opportunity.

Carpe diem—seize the day.

'Absolutely,' she said with resolution. 'By the scruff of the neck—if I can find the courage.'

'I gather I'm conveying a ball gown to London on Friday when I go down for this conference,' Owen said on the phone later.

'If I can make it in time. I've got so much to do—including another Law essay for tomorrow night.'

'You're nuts,' he told her, for the third or fourth time. 'Anyway, what sort of dress? Haven't you got one in stock that would do?'

'Oh, yes. I've got one she wants, but she's not having it. That gold one you pulled out,' she told him, and he nearly choked down the phone.

'Good grief! Can this be your daughter?'

'I don't know,' Cait said worriedly. 'I'm just beginning

to wonder that myself. The worrying thing is, maybe she's more like her mother than is good for her.'

'Oh, come on, now, don't be hard on yourself because you made a mistake when you were a kid,' he said softly, and she sighed.

'I'll die if she throws her life away like I did.'

'You didn't throw it away,' he corrected. 'You spent it doing something wonderful—you gave Milly her life. Don't underrate that.'

'And she's just told me I've wasted enough of my life and I should go for it.'

'Go for what?' he asked, sounding puzzled, and she told him about the conversation she'd had with her daughter about her whereabouts the night before.

Owen laughed without humour. 'I haven't told Josh. I don't have your courage.'

'I didn't *tell* Milly,' she said drily. 'She guessed. She said I sounded different. I don't know if she believed me when I said nothing happened. I just felt sick telling her. I'm so afraid she'll judge me.'

'Don't be afraid,' he murmured. 'She won't—and even if she does in the short term, at the end of the day she'll realise all you've done for her and she'll come round. They need to grow up before they can deal with complex adult emotions.'

They're not alone, Cait thought as she struggled to rough out a design for Milly's dress that evening. She was dealing with some pretty complex emotions herself, and she was way out of her depth.

She loved Owen, of that she was sure. Whether he loved her or not was highly debatable. If he did—or even, come to that, if he didn't—why hadn't he made love to her last night? Heaven knows, she was more than willing, and she wouldn't have put up much of a fight.

Perhaps that was the trouble. Maybe he liked his women sober and co-operative, not falling asleep and stumbling drunkenly around. She just hoped she hadn't disgraced herself. She didn't think she had, but her judgement was a bit iffy and her memory was probably not entirely accurate.

'Never again,' she mumbled through a mouthful of pins, and stood back to look at her mock-up.

It would do fine, she thought. A little tuck here, perhaps—yes, that was better. She rummaged through her fabrics, found something black and electric blue in a striking shot silk effect that would look stunning on her dark-haired daughter, and by the time she went to bed she'd put it together and hung it on the model to drop, so she could hem it the next day.

Success. All she had to do now was her Law essay!

'So this is it, then?'

'Yes. Try not to crease it—even though she'll throw it on the floor once she's worn it, and I expect someone will spill something down it within the first five minutes.'

'Or worse. Half of them had alcohol poisoning after Saturday night, apparently,' he told her.

'I am not going to presume to criticise,' Cait said piously, and he laughed.

'You were a very long way off alcohol poisoning.'

'It didn't feel like that on Sunday morning.'

'You were fine. You were just a bit tiddly. I'm still feeling guilty.'

'Good,' she said, firmly squashing her smile. 'When will you be back from London?'

'Oh, late,' Owen said with a sigh. 'Friday night traffic is hideous. I thought I might avoid it and take Josh out for dinner. He said I could doss on his bed and he'll sleep on the floor, but I think I need my creature comforts and, anyway, I have to get back for the dogs—unless you want to sleep there for me?'

'I have to open the shop on Saturday,' she reminded him, and he nodded.

'That's fine. I'll come back tomorrow night late. Mrs Poole can go in and feed them at five, and they'll be fine till I get home.'

'Ring me when you get back—tell me how she looks,' she said, and wondered if her voice was really as mournful as it seemed to her.

'She'll be fine. I might be very late.'

'Still, please, ring. I want to know you're safely home.'

His eyes flickered with something she couldn't quite read, and he put the dress down carefully and drew her into his arms.

'I have to go now,' he said, cradling her against his body. 'I've got work to do before I can leave tomorrow.'

'I might do my next Law assignment so I don't have to stay up all Sunday night again,' she mumbled into his shirt, and then she breathed in deeply and sighed with contentment. He smelt warm and familiar and absolutely right, a combination of soap and man that was utterly intoxicating.

Maybe that was what had pushed her over the edge on Saturday?

Owen lifted his head and smiled at her tenderly. 'I have to go.'

She nodded, and went up on tiptoe to kiss him goodbye. 'Don't forget the dress,' she reminded him, 'or Cinderella won't be going to the ball.'

'Cinderella? Milly? Not a chance. By all accounts she hasn't missed a single evening out—unlike her mother.'

'Oh, her mother's fine. Although…' Cait tipped her head on one side and looked up at him with an ironic smile

'...you know something? You know what I do for a living? I make and hire out ball gowns. And do you know I have never once, in my entire life, been to a ball? Isn't that the silliest thing you ever heard?'

He gave a slow, lazy smile, and pulled something from his pocket. 'That's just about to change,' he told her. 'Saturday week—in Audley. It's a fundraiser for the League of Friends of the hospital. I bought two tickets. So, *Cinderella*, you shall go to the ball!'

CHAPTER EIGHT

'YOU'VE taken your wedding ring off.'

Owen glanced down at his finger, still strangely bare and feeling very naked, and nodded.

'Yes, I have.'

'Have you got a woman?'

He looked at his son, trying to read his feelings and failing hopelessly. 'I have met someone, yes.'

Josh looked away, his eyes veiled. 'I wondered if you would, when I went away.'

'It wasn't planned.'

The boy shrugged, and Owen got the distinct impression he was trying to hide his hurt.

'Josh, it's just coincidence. I didn't deliberately go out of my way to find someone the moment you were gone, but I met her, and the time seemed right.'

'Are you sleeping together?'

He felt the shock of the question right down to his toes, and almost glanced over his shoulder to see if anyone else in the crowded restaurant had heard. It seemed unlikely.

'Not that I think it's any of your business,' he said in a low voice, 'but, no, I'm not. Not yet, at least.'

'But you might.'

'I might.'

Josh speared him with a penetrating stare. 'Would Mum approve of her?'

He thought of Jill and Cait, so different and yet in many ways so similar, and he nodded slowly. 'Yes, I think so.'

'That's all right, then. Just so long as you're happy.'

'I am,' Owen said, and realised as he spoke that it was true. 'I'm happier than I've been for years.'

'Good.' Josh changed the subject, obviously uncomfortable with it, and Owen eased out a sigh of relief and settled down to listen to the catalogue of wild parties and endless shenanigans the freshers had got up to since they'd last spoken.

Good grief, he thought, Cait and I are going to have to get a great deal wilder to compete with that lot!

'Just don't spend *all* your money on alcohol,' he cautioned, which was a rash thing to do, because he ended up shelling out for a set of textbooks that cost more than he would have believed possible.

Ah, well, he thought, it's only money. And then he wondered how Cait would provide for Milly, and thought again just how much she'd sacrificed to give the girl her chance in life.

Suddenly he couldn't wait to get back to her.

'Will I do?'

Cait twirled in front of him, the new gown she'd just completed swirling out around her and settling back with a silken whisper against her skin.

It was a wonderful deep sapphire colour, perfect with her colouring, and it made her skin look like alabaster. Owen felt his body surge to life, and cleared his throat.

'You look lovely,' he said, his voice sounding strained to his ears, and she smiled diffidently and coloured, a soft wash of pale rose tinting her skin and bringing her to life. Lord, she was gorgeous. He hardly dared trust himself to touch her, but he helped her into her coat with fingers that trembled to caress her skin, and when he brushed her shoulder accidentally with the back of his hand, heat shot through him.

'I've got my overnight things,' she said, and he nodded curtly.

'Fine. Let's go, then. The taxi's picking us up from home in fifteen minutes.'

He hardly had time to put her bag in the spare room before the taxi beeped outside, and he ran down, patted the dogs absently and ushered her out.

It was a clear night, crisp and cold, and he knew it would freeze later. He'd lit the fire—partly for the dogs, and partly so they would have a focus of warmth when they came back so they could sit up and drink coffee and talk into the wee small hours of the night.

He wasn't thinking beyond that, wasn't letting his mind or his imagination run away with him. He didn't dare. One thing at a time, he told himself. One thing at a time.

The ball was everything Cait might have hoped for and more. Everyone was elegantly turned out, and she recognised some of her dresses in the crowd.

While Owen was getting them drinks, one of her regulars saw her and did a mild double take. 'Cait?' she said, and smiled a broad welcome. 'We don't usually see you at these things! How nice to see you on the other side of the counter, as it were. What a gorgeous dress!'

She turned to the tall and rather striking man beside her. 'Darling, this is Cait Cooper—she's got that wonderful ball gown hire shop in Wenham, and she makes the most fabulous dresses. She's amazing. Oh, that sounds so patronising, but it isn't meant to be, Cait. You really are so talented. I can't believe how lucky we are to have you.'

'Aren't we?' Owen said, coming up behind her. 'Cait, allow me to introduce you to Ryan and Ginny O'Connor. By the sound of it you've met Ginny before, and Ryan's someone I hope you'll never meet professionally—he's one of our A and E consultants.'

'Ah! Right. Hi, there,' she said, laughing softly at Owen's introduction and shaking Ryan's hand. 'It's nice to meet you. I hardly ever get to meet the husbands.'

'They're cheated,' he said gallantly in a soft Canadian burr, and he winked at her. 'I shall have to make a point of coming along for fittings in future.'

'If you're allowed,' Ginny retorted. 'It's a girly thing, usually, isn't it, Cait?'

'Only because men get bored to death. They just don't have our stamina.'

'You can say that again,' Ryan groaned. He slid an arm round his wife's waist and drew her closer. 'How about that dance you promised me?' he murmured, and Ginny smiled at Cait and Owen and excused herself, and they went off towards the dance floor.

Cait's eyes followed them longingly. She'd never danced anywhere except at a nightclub or a disco, and that only a very few times in her life. Certainly she'd never danced in a long, floaty dress with a man's arms around her as he whirled her round the floor.

'Sounds like a good idea.' Owen's voice was soft, his breath teasing her skin. He was still standing slightly behind her, and his hands came up and cupped her shoulders, bringing a shiver of anticipation to her skin. 'What do you think?'

'I think it sounds like a lovely idea,' she said a trifle breathlessly, and turned towards him. 'Could we?'

Heavens, was she really as wistful as she sounded? Owen's eyes creased in a smile. 'I'm sure we could.' He cupped her elbow with his hand and led her to the dance floor, then turned her into his arms.

'I don't think I can remember any of the fancy things,' she told him, and he chuckled.

'I never knew them. Just relax. I won't know if you do it wrong, and if you're very careful I probably won't tread on you more than a few times.'

He didn't tread on her at all, and Cait was sure he was lying about not knowing the steps. She didn't care. She just rested one hand on his shoulder, placed her other hand in his and let him guide her. At first he kept a discreet distance between them, but gradually they settled closer together, until her head was on his shoulder and their clasped hands were tucked in against their bodies, so that the back of his hand brushed her breast.

She could feel the shift of his thighs against hers as they moved slowly to the music, and after a while her steadily building awareness threatened to consume her. To an outsider they would have appeared just like any other couple dancing, she thought, and yet she could feel the tension humming in him, the savagely suppressed passion simmering just below the surface, like a banked furnace.

Finally the master of ceremonies called the last dance, and she could feel the tension in him mounting to unbearable levels. Then the music swirled to a halt with a flourish, the band were sent off to thunderous applause and Owen eased away from her and looked down into her eyes.

'Time to go,' he said gruffly, and she could see the desire burning in his eyes.

They were silent in the taxi, and when they arrived back at the house he put the dogs out, then filled the kettle and put it on the Aga.

'Coffee?' he asked, and Cait lifted her shoulders in a tiny shrug.

'If you want.'

Their eyes met and locked. 'You know what I want,' he said, his voice low and taut with emotion.

She smiled a little unsteadily. 'So what are you waiting for, Owen?' she murmured.

He closed his eyes briefly and then opened them again, and she almost staggered under the force of the need that blazed from them. 'Dogs,' he said distractedly, and went to the back door, calling them in.

He threw them a biscuit each, took the kettle off the hob and held out his hand. 'Come to bed,' he said softly, and her legs nearly gave way.

Reaching out her hand, she placed it in his, her trust in him absolute. She had never loved like this before, and she knew she never would again. As her hand linked with his, so did her heart and soul, and in that moment she gave herself to him completely.

The sun streaming in through the window woke Owen, and he propped himself up on one elbow and looked down at Cait. She was beautiful—her skin warm and flushed with sleep, her lashes like dark crescents against her rose-petal cheeks.

Her lips were slightly swollen from their kisses, and there was a touch of whisker-burn on her lip. He leant over and kissed it better, and her lashes fluttered up and she smiled at him.

'Hi,' she said, her voice shy and tentative, and he smiled back and kissed her again.

'Hi yourself. How are you?'

'Wonderful,' she told him, her eyes shining. 'How are you?'

'Likewise.' He eased the quilt away from her shoulders and looked down at her, at the soft dusky rose of her nipples puckering in the cool air, the smooth swell of her breasts, the flat plain of her stomach. She was beautiful, and he felt desire rip through him again.

He'd been right when he'd thought she'd be amazing to make love to. Her face was a mirror of her feelings, every touch, every stroke of his hands registering in her expressive features.

He kissed her again, and she reached for him, drawing him into her arms, and he was lost.

Cait had never been so happy. She'd thought she'd known what to expect, but afterwards she realised that her slight and very limited experience hadn't prepared her at all for the love-making of a skilled and patient man. Every touch had registered, every kiss had found its target, and when he took her home on Sunday night, she felt more cherished and loved than she'd ever felt in her entire life.

Nevertheless, at the back of her mind she worried that they hadn't taken any precautions, and so on Monday morning she went to see Max Carter, her GP.

'I don't think there's the slightest danger that I'm pregnant,' she told him frankly, 'because it's right at the end of my cycle, but I ought to go on the Pill for the future, I think.'

He nodded. 'I can give you a prescription for the morning-after pill as it's called, if you like, but you don't sound as if you think it's necessary, and it's getting a bit late now for it to be effective anyway. It's up to you.'

She shook her head. 'No. I'm sure I'm safe. I'm as regular as clockwork. I know I can't be pregnant.'

So he checked her over and gave her a prescription for the Pill, and she started taking it straight away to give her cover immediately after her period was over.

Except that it didn't come. The week passed, and Milly came home for the weekend and slept for most of it because she was so exhausted, and Cait cooked for her and tried not to think about what was happening inside her.

Perhaps it was because of the Pill, she thought, and ignored the nagging doubt. Not that she needed to be on the Pill, as it turned out, because she hardly saw Owen.

First, Milly and Josh were both up for the weekend, and then he had to go away to a conference, but she didn't really have time to miss him because she was into a frenzy with the Christmas ball rush starting and everyone panicking about their dresses.

He spoke to her on the phone from Italy, though, almost every day, and because she was so busy trying to ignore the time bomb that was going off inside her, she told him all about her Law course and how well it was going, and how she planned another course for the following year— maybe a residential course for a few weeks at a quiet time of the year, if she could afford it.

'That's great,' he said, sounding quite enthusiastic, and she thought, Oh, lord, he doesn't care if I go away. I wonder what he's doing in Italy, and with whom?

She threw herself back into the ball gowns, ignoring Owen and her missing period and her sudden loss of interest in tea and coffee.

Then finally she could ignore it no longer, because she woke up on the Tuesday morning just over two weeks after the ball, went into the bathroom with a pregnancy test kit and came face to face with her worst nightmare.

'You idiot!' she berated herself, tears streaming down her face. 'How could you have been such a fool? Twice, for goodness' sake!'

She thought of Emily, of the struggle she'd had to bring her up, the endless nights walking the floor with her and then trying to work during the day while her daughter slept; she remembered their flat, cold in winter and hot in summer and damp all year round, and she wrapped her arms round her waist and rocked her baby and sobbed as if her heart would break, because she loved its father and he didn't love her, and there was no way she could do anything but have it, and she was going right back to square one, her life in tatters all over again.

She went out of the bathroom and picked up the phone, staring at it blankly. Owen had rung at three o'clock in the morning to say he was back from his conference in Italy, and he wanted to see her again that night. Good, because she needed to see him, and suddenly she couldn't wait till the end of the day. She punched in his number, and he answered on the third ring, sounding sleepy and sexy and wonderful.

Except that he thought it was a good idea for her to go away on a Law course for a few weeks or months or whatever.

Oh, lord.

'I need to see you,' she said, her hand trembling. The little indicator strip was mocking her, and she put it down before she dropped it. 'Can I come round now?'

'Now?' he said, and she could hear the bedclothes rustling. 'Um—sure. Just give me half an hour to shower and dress.'

She couldn't wait that long. She got into her car, drove round to his house and sat outside, twisting her hands on the steering wheel until he opened the door and came out.

Her courage deserted her, and she sat there watching him as he crossed the gravel drive and pulled open her door, hunkering down beside her and taking her hands in his, his face worried.

'Cait?' he said softly. 'Darling, what's the matter? Is it Milly?'

She dragged in a shuddering breath. 'I need to talk to you.'

He straightened up, still holding her hand, and helped her out of the car. 'Come inside,' he said gently, and led her in, closing the door behind her and turning her into his arms.

She stood stiffly, her body frozen with shock and dread and the terrible acceptance of defeat, because she knew she was going to lose him, and she couldn't make her mouth say the words that would take him away from her for ever.

After a moment he dropped his arms and stepped back, looking down at her with his hands on her shoulders, steadying her as one shudder after another ripped through her frame.

'Cait, for God's sake, talk to me,' he said unsteadily, his voice ragged. 'What's wrong with you? What is it? Oh, God, tell me you're not dying.'

'Dying?' she said, freed suddenly from the immobility that had gripped her for the past few minutes. 'No, I'm not dying, Owen,' she said hollowly. 'I'm pregnant.'

CHAPTER NINE

'PREGNANT?'

Owen's hands fell to his sides, and he stabbed his fingers through his hair. His hand was trembling, Cait noticed absently, and any moment now he'd tell her she was trying to trick him into supporting her, and throw her out, as Robert and his father had done. She steeled herself for the blow—but it didn't fall.

Not yet, at least.

Finally he moved. 'Come and sit down,' he said gently, and led her through to the sitting room. 'Tea? Coffee?'

She shook her head, a shudder of distaste rippling through her. 'No, please. Nothing.'

She stood there, and he took her shoulders and pressed softly on them until her knees gave way and she sat down on one end of the sofa with a plop, then he sat at the other end, one leg hitched up, his elbow propped on the back, his head supported on his hand, watching her.

'I take it this isn't good news?' he said eventually, and she stared at him as if he were mad.

'Good news?' She laughed, and her voice cracked. 'How can it be good news?' she asked, close to hysteria. 'I've only just got Emily off my hands, I was just about to start my life! I'm thirty-five, Owen. I'll be fifty-three by the time this baby leaves for university—no, fifty-four! That's ancient! That's almost all my working life! I was going to have a career...'

Cait put down the hem of her sweater before she tore it in half, and bit her knuckle instead.

'Doing Law,' he said flatly.

'Something to do with it, probably.'

'Why?'

'Why?' She looked at him as if he had two heads. 'Because I've always wanted to do Law!'

'OK, so you want to do Law. What about your shop?'

She shrugged. 'I don't know. I can't afford to give it up, not for years, probably. I might have to pay for help so I can study.'

Owen nodded. 'And where does the baby fit into all this?'

She rolled her eyes. 'It doesn't! That's the whole *point*! The baby is just—I can't believe I was that stupid. All these years I've waited for my freedom, and the first half-decent man to come along and I throw it all away.'

'Was that supposed to be a compliment?' he interrupted, and his smile was strained.

She closed her eyes, the fight going out of her. 'I'm sorry. I didn't mean it like that. You've been wonderful to me, and it's been the best time of my life, but now I'm going to have to pay for it, like I always have to pay, and it's just so damned unfair.'

'Don't do anything silly, will you?' he said carefully, and there was an edge in his voice that made her look at him more closely.

'Silly? You mean have an abortion? You think that's what this is all about?'

'I don't know,' he said quietly. 'I hope not. If it is, then if there's anything I can do to change your mind—I'll have the baby when it's born, bring it up, look after it, pay all its expenses—anything you want, Cait. Just don't kill my baby, please. I'll do anything rather than stand back and let you do that.'

Anything except marry me, she thought hollowly. Tell me you love me, Owen. Tell me you're overjoyed. Tell me anything, just don't sit there and be so bloody reasonable and try and negotiate.

'I don't want anything from you,' she lied. 'You can have access, of course you can, and see it as much as you want, but I don't want your money.' Just your heart.

'Can I see it every day? Every night?'

She stared at him, puzzled. 'Every day?'

'Yes. You said I could see it as much as I wanted. That's every day, Cait. I want to see my baby born. I want to see it grow up. I want to be there when it takes its first step, and kiss it better when it falls down. I'm not going to be an absentee father—not unless you make me.'

Owen reached out, taking her cold and lifeless hand in his warm, strong, vital one. 'Marry me, Cait,' he said, his voice vibrating with emotion. 'Marry me and live here with me and our baby. Be a family.'

It was such a wonderful thought that she nearly agreed, but then she remembered how he'd encouraged her to go away on the residential course she'd talked about, almost as if she'd become too much of a fixture in his life.

And the last thing she wanted was to be a burden to him, a duty, so she and her child became a sea-anchor weighing him down and ruining his life so that he ended up hating them both.

'You don't mean that. You're only saying it because you're afraid I'll kill it.'

'No.'

'Yes.' Cait dredged up a smile. 'It's all right, Owen, I'm not going to do anything stupid. You don't have to do the decent thing, as they say. I'm only telling you because I think you have a right to know.'

'So you won't marry me?'

She shook her head. 'It wouldn't work.'

'It might.' He glanced at his watch, then stood up.

'Look, I'm sorry, I have to go to the hospital. They rang just after you did and they've got a crisis on. I can't get out of it, or I would, because we have to talk this through. I'll come and see you tonight as soon as I get away, and in the meantime think about it. Think about the advantages and disadvantages of marrying me, and we'll talk again tonight. OK?'

She stood up. 'I won't change my mind, Owen,' she warned, and he gave her a grim little smile.

'Just take the time. Please. That's all I ask. Take the time, think about it and let me know your answer.'

She nodded in the end, because it was the easiest thing to do, and then she went home, opened up the shop and sat down at the desk with a piece of paper.

She wrote at the top 'Advantages' and 'Disadvantages', then wrote down all the pros and cons in the two columns.

At the end of the exercise one thing was clear. The advantages outweighed the disadvantages by about a hundred to one, but the one disadvantage was too huge to overcome.

'He'll hate me,' she'd written in shaky script, and even as she read it, her eyes filled and welled over, and she laid her head down on the desk and wept.

'Cait? Oh, dear, love, what's the matter?'

She dragged in a deep breath and sat up, scrubbing the tears from her cheeks. The lady who ran the antique shop next door was hovering by her desk, her eyes concerned. Cait dredged up a smile. 'Oh, hello, Gilda. I'm sorry, I was just having a wallow.'

'Oh, Cait. Missing Milly, I expect, are you? I remember when mine went away—awful. Just awful.'

Cait sniffed and nodded. She couldn't tell Gilda what was wrong—not now, before she'd got all her ducks in a row and decided what she was doing.

Although only an idiot would turn Owen down.

'Oh! You're not wearing it!'

'What?' She blinked at Gilda, who was staring dumbstruck at her hand. 'Wearing what?'

'Um—oh, nothing. A—a dress I thought you were wearing today, but you're not. I've just realised—Cait, I have to go, love. I just saw you through the window, and—well, take care. Come and have a chat if you want.'

Gilda patted her awkwardly on the shoulder and almost ran out, leaving Cait totally confused. What on earth was she on about?

She looked at her clothes, a plain pencil skirt and a neat blouse, with a comfy old cardigan snuggled over the top because the shop was always chilly until the sun came round, and shook her head. Gilda had really lost it.

She looked back down at her list, splodged with tears, and felt a sob welling in her chest. What on earth was she to do? Marry him, even though he was only doing it for the baby, or struggle on alone sharing her—or him—with Owen, scrapping about Christmas and birthdays and school holidays, with the poor little mite being passed from pillar to post?

At least Milly had had absolute security. They may have had nothing else, but her daughter had always known her mother would be there for her come hell or high water, at any hour of the day or night, and there had never been any question of how much she loved her.

'Oh, damn,' she said, and shut the list into her desk drawer. She had too much to do to waste time in useless contemplation. She'd talk to Owen tonight and, depending on what he said, she'd make a decision.

And, please, God, she thought, let it be the right one...

* * *

Owen struggled through a difficult day with an enormous effort of will. He was tired after the conference, suffering from lack of sleep, and standing in a hot theatre all day battling to save one life after another after a major incident was not his idea of a restful first day back.

Still, it occupied his mind totally, which was what he needed in the absence of being able to go and deal with his dilemma immediately.

Dilemma? he thought, and shook his head. No, not a dilemma. Well, not the baby, anyway. That wasn't a dilemma, it was a wonderful and precious gift, something he'd thought would never happen to him again. After Josh, he and Jill had never taken steps to prevent another pregnancy, but nothing had happened.

Jill hadn't really minded, but Owen had ached for another child for years, and it had only been when Jill had died that he'd finally resigned himself.

And now Cait was having his baby, and because she'd convinced herself she wanted to do something with Law, of all the dry and tedious things to want to study, she was seeing this precious gift of their child as a burden.

Well, he'd have to find a way to persuade her otherwise, so he could keep her safe and love and cherish her and their child till the end of his days.

If the stubborn, silly woman would only let him.

'Retractors,' he snapped, and the scrub nurse beside him gave him a long-suffering look and slapped them in his hand. 'Sorry,' he mumbled, and her eyebrows shot up.

'You're like a bear with a sore head today,' she said under her breath. 'If I were you, I'd have a hot toddy and an early night.'

He snorted softly. If only it were that simple.

*   *   *

Owen rang Cait at six to say he was back at home and would like to see her.

She looked around her flat, horribly untidy because she'd been working late every night this week and had hardly given it a glance, and wanted to weep with frustration. At the very least, she wanted to have the place clean and tidy so he didn't start accusing her of being a slut and an unfit mother.

'I thought,' he went on, 'if you don't mind and haven't got any other plans, maybe I could get a taxi to pick you up and bring you here for a meal.'

So she was off the hook as far as the housework went, anyway. 'I don't know if I can eat,' she said worriedly, nausea nibbling at her even as she spoke.

'Don't worry about eating. You can have something simple. I just—Cait, give me a chance,' he said softly, and if she hadn't known better, she would have thought he really cared.

'I'll drive over,' she said.

'You don't need to do that,' he protested, but she cut him off.

'Yes, I do,' she corrected. 'I'm all right to drive. I'm pregnant, Owen, not crippled. I'll see you later. What time?'

'Seven?'

She looked at her watch and sighed. 'OK. I'll see you then.'

Pride made her dress up. Pride and a perverse urge to make him want her, even though she knew he didn't, not really. He was still in love with his wife, and she'd been a fool to imagine that she could have a part in his life.

She wore the black dress he'd liked the first time they'd gone out, even though it was ridiculously over the top for the occasion, and she put on slinky tights and high, strappy

sandals that were totally impractical to drive in but made
her legs look as if they went on for ever.

As an afterthought she put down extra food for Bagpuss,
who was getting fat and bossy and more demanding than
ever now Milly was gone, and she put on her best coat,
courtesy of the Oxfam shop, and drove over to Owen's,
arriving just a few seconds after seven.

He opened the door immediately and came over to the
car to help her out. He was dressed in casual trousers and
a cream cashmere sweater that set off his wonderful toffee-
coloured eyes, and he scanned her with them as she
stepped out of the car and for the briefest moment heat
flared in them.

Good, she thought. She felt more confident knowing she
still had some power over him, because she felt terrifyingly
powerless in this situation. Not that it was about power,
but the balance was firmly in his favour, and whatever
happened she was going to be the loser once again.

Her hand slid down over her abdomen. No, not the loser,
she thought. Never that, my little one. Not with you.

Owen took her elbow and helped her across the gravel,
and because she was wearing those ridiculous shoes she
let him. She got a stone in the toe, but she said nothing,
just pasted on a smile and kept walking, and he took her
into the house and settled her in the sitting room.

The fire was lit, and the dogs wagged their tails but
didn't bother to move. It was too warm and comfortable,
and she didn't blame them.

'Can I get you a drink?'

Cait looked up into his eyes, shadowed now because his
back was to the light, and wished she could read his ex-
pression. 'Please. Could I have water?'

'I've got mineral water—fizzy, with ice and lemon?'

It sounded wonderful. 'Please.'

He went up to the kitchen, and she surreptitiously slipped her shoe off and removed the stone, then put it back on just as he returned with a tall glass in each hand.

'How was work?' she asked, throwing him, and he gave a short laugh and dropped onto the other end of the sofa.

'Horrendous. There was a gas explosion in a factory. That's why they called me in. I spent the day gluing people together again, not always successfully.'

'I'm sorry.'

'Mmm. Whatever.' He stared down into his glass, shadows chasing across his face, and she knew he was reliving the horrors of the day. Then he turned to her, his eyes searching her face, and his mouth twitched into a fleeting smile. 'Sorry. I haven't even asked about you. How are you? How was your day? Are you OK?'

'Sick. Busy.' *Sad because you don't love me.*

'I'm sorry—about the baby. I feel so guilty about this, because I should really have thought about it when we made love, but—well, Jill and I never needed to. After Josh she didn't get pregnant again, and I suppose I've just stopped thinking about it.'

'Most woman are on the Pill,' she said in mitigation.

'You'd think I'd remember, but I didn't even think about it. I suppose it's been such a long time—it isn't something I do,' she explained, wondering if it was possible to become a virgin again after eighteen years, because that was what she'd felt like.

'No—I don't, either. It was the first time since Jill died. It just didn't seem right before, but somehow, with you—' He broke off, staring down into his glass again, and she wondered if he had a script concealed in it, little flashcards with key words on.

Oh, lord.

'I wasn't expecting it to be so beautiful,' he said softly,

and his words nearly reduced her to tears. 'I thought it would be messy and difficult and I'd feel bad afterwards, but it wasn't and I didn't, and if we had to conceive a child, then to have done it that night seems somehow right.'

He put his glass down and took hers away, moving closer to her and taking her hand in his.

'Cait, I know this isn't what you wanted from your life, but it's happening, and we have to make the best of it. I don't know what you want to do, but if there's any way I can help, I will. If you want to go away and take a degree, I'll get a nanny to look after the baby and you can come home at weekends and in the holidays, and we'll manage somehow, if it's what you want.

'Or if you just want to carry on running your shop, you could let the flat and run it from here, or expand it upstairs into the flat, or move to another shop nearer—whatever. And Milly—there'll always be room for Milly here with you, you know that, don't you? Or if you just want to stop work and stay at home with the baby—whatever you want, whatever would make you happy.'

Owen trailed off, and she realised his eyes were glazed with tears. Oh, lord, she thought, he really wants this baby. If he and Jill never had any more and he wanted them, no wonder he's so desperate to have it here.

'You could even have the spare room, if you'd rather. We could divide off one end of it to make a nursery, and you and the baby could share it. Or you could have Josh's rooms and be even more separate, if you would rather.'

'What do you want?' she asked. 'Apart from the baby?'

'You,' he said after a long pause. 'I want you, Cait. I love you. I was going to ask you to marry me tonight, when I came back from Italy. I'd got a ring and everything.

Then you started talking about going away, and I suddenly wasn't sure if you would want me.'

His voice cracked slightly, and Cait felt a great well of love building up inside her. 'Owen, of course I want you!' she said raggedly. 'I don't care about my course! It's boring. I just thought—I don't know, I'd thought about it for such a long time, and there it was. I was only doing it because I'd been planning it for years, but I don't want to go away. I don't want to do anything except have your baby and live here with you. I just didn't think you'd want me.'

'Not want you?' he said, stunned. 'Cait, how could I not want you? You're warm and funny and brave and beautiful—what is there about you not to want?'

'I can't cook,' she said, laughing tearfully. 'And I'm a lousy housewife.'

'That's fine. So am I. I have a housekeeper for that very reason.'

'And I'm an unmarried mother, and in your position in the community—'

'What position?' he said, his voice disgusted. 'People don't care about that sort of thing any more. Anyway, if I have anything to say about it you won't be an unmarried mother for very much longer.'

He slipped his hand into his pocket and pulled out a little ring, diamonds and sapphires in a very old setting, the light sparkling off the stones and dazzling her through her tears. 'I got it from Gilda next door. I told her it was for you. I didn't tell her why, but I think she guessed.'

Cait remembered Gilda that morning, staring at her hand and mumbling something about a dress. 'That's what she was on about,' she said slowly. 'I saw her this morning. She obviously expected that I'd be wearing it, but I wasn't. I was crying over a list of pros and cons—well, pros, actually. There was only one con, and I don't think it applies.'

'What was it?' he asked.

She took a deep breath. 'I thought you'd hate me, after a while. I'd be in your house, untidying everything, the baby would be screaming, you'd be tired and fed up with us all, and I thought you'd start to wonder why on earth you'd agreed to it. But maybe you won't.'

'Not a chance,' he said, taking her hand and slipping the ring onto her finger. It was a perfect fit, a tiny bit on the loose side if anything, but that was probably as well as she was pregnant and her fingers might swell.

'You haven't actually asked me to marry you yet,' she reminded him. 'Not properly. Not for the right reasons.'

'I haven't? How remiss.'

He slid off the sofa onto his knees, took her hand in his and stared deep into her eyes. 'I love you, Cait,' he said carefully, every word clear so she couldn't possibly mistake it. 'I think I've loved you since I found you crying over your steering-wheel in the car park the day we took the kids to uni. I don't know if you love me. I hope you do, or that you'll learn to, because I know I'll love you till the day I die. Marry me, Cait. Let's be a family—a real family, all five of us. God knows, we all deserve it.'

Owen reached out a hand and brushed the tears from her cheeks with his knuckles. 'Marry me, my darling. Please?'

She nodded, unable to speak, and then she swallowed hard and took a steadying breath. 'Of course I'll marry you—and of course I love you, you idiot!' she said, and then she was in his arms, wrapped hard against his chest, her mascara ruining the front of his beautiful cashmere sweater. 'Oh, look what I've done,' she said wretchedly when he straightened up.

'Forget it. You can cry all over everything I own for all I care. It's all yours anyway.' He pulled her to her feet, tutted and pushed her down again, then took off her ridiculous shoes. 'You can't walk in these, you'll mess your back up,' he said crossly, and lifted her into his arms.

'Where are you taking me?' she said curiously.

'Bed,' he replied. 'I'm tired. I want to lie down somewhere comfortable and hold you and listen to you telling me you love me until I fall asleep in your arms.'

'What a lovely idea. What about supper?'

'You want to eat, too?' he said, and put her down again. 'You're pregnant, aren't you, of course.'

She nodded.

'Pregnant women are always unreasonable. I should have remembered that.' He made a detour into the kitchen, picked up the biscuit tin and a bottle of mineral water and handed them to her, then scooped all of them up into his arms and carried her up to bed.

'You're looking very smug,' she remarked as he put her down in the middle of the bed.

'Am I?' Owen sat down beside her, his face suddenly serious. 'I don't mean to be. When Jill died, I thought I'd lost everything, and when Josh went away I felt as if I'd come to the end of the road. I was just thirty-nine, and there was nothing left for me except my career—and then I met you. You've given me my life back, Cait. You've given me love and laughter, and another family to look forward to—a baby I thought I'd never have, a teenage daughter to test my patience and a beautiful woman to walk beside me through our lives. Can you blame me for looking just a tiny bit smug?'

His smile was gentle and a little sad, and she swallowed hard and hugged him.

'No. No, I can't. I feel the same.'

His eyes darkened and, taking the biscuits and the water away from her, he lay down beside her and took her into his arms. 'I love you,' he said softly, and kissed her...

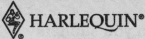

If you enjoyed what you just read,
then we've got an offer you can't resist!

Take 2 bestselling
love stories FREE!

Plus get a FREE surprise gift!